I'M TRAPPED IN
A VAMPIRE'S BODY

Other books by Todd Strasser

I'M TRAPPED IN
A VAMPIRE'S BODY

TODD STRASSER

AN
APPLE
PAPERBACK

SCHOLASTIC INC.

New York Toronto London Auckland Sydney
Mexico City New Delhi Hong Kong

ISBN 0-439-21034-8

12 11 10 9 8 7 6 5 4 3 2 1   0 1 2 3 4 5/0

Printed in the U.S.A.   40

First Scholastic printing, October 2000

For the Hundleys

I'M TRAPPED IN
A VAMPIRE'S BODY

1

"**D**o you think you and Jake will be okay?" my mom asked.

"Oh, sure," I heard my sister answer.

It was breakfasttime on the day before Halloween, and I was coming down the hall. Mom and Jessica were already in the kitchen. I stopped and listened. They didn't know I was there.

"I just don't know." Mom sounded worried. "I hope we're not doing the wrong thing."

"Believe me, Mom, Jake will live through Halloween," my sister said. "You may have to bail him out of jail when you and Dad get back from Chicago, but at least he'll still have two arms and two legs."

Chicago? I thought.

"Of course," Jessica went on, "I can't promise he'll have all his fingers. But he could probably get along without a few."

"That's not very reassuring," Mom said.

"I'm just kidding, Mom," I heard Jessica answer. "Everything will be fine."

"Definitely," I said, and stepped into the kitchen.

Mom and Jessica turned and looked at me with surprised expressions. Our dog, Lance, got to his feet and came over, wagging his tail and eager for me to scratch him behind the ears.

"Were you listening?" Mom asked. She was wearing her workclothes, a white blouse and a blue skirt and jacket.

"Maybe," I said.

My sister was wearing a tight white T-shirt and baggy plaid pajama bottoms. Jessica's newest thing was kickboxing in the gym every day after school so she could have a hard body and feel like she could beat up the world.

"What's this about Chicago?" I asked.

"Dad and I are supposed to go away for Halloween," Mom explained.

"Oh?" I tried not to act too excited. Halloween was tomorrow.

"It's Uncle Bobby's fiftieth birthday, and Aunt Rachel is throwing him a surprise party," Mom said. "Your father and I feel that you and Jessica are now old enough to be left on your own. But we need to know that you won't do anything that will disappoint us while we're gone."

Mom and Dad were trying a new tactic. Instead of getting mad and punishing me when I got into trouble, they'd just say that I'd "disappointed" them. In other words, Mom was saying that she and Dad would be disappointed if I burned down the house or blew up the dog or locked Jessica in the garage with a dead skunk.

Not that I would *ever* do anything like that.

But if Mom and Dad were going away for Halloween, I *might* just throw the best Halloween party ever.

"So?" Mom wanted to know if she could trust me.

"I won't disappoint you, Mom," I promised. "I intend to have a quiet Halloween with a few of my closest friends."

Mom gave me an uncertain look. Then she checked her watch. "I have to go to work, kids. We'll talk more about this at dinner. Bye."

She went down the hall and out the front door. Jessica turned and said, "A quiet Halloween with a few of your closest friends? That's about as likely as — "

"You getting a date for the prom?" I guessed.

Jessica gritted her teeth angrily at me. "I'm going upstairs to get dressed."

As soon as Jessica left the kitchen, I got on the phone and called my friend Josh Hopka.

"Yeah?" Josh answered with a yawn.

"It's party time," I said.

3

2

"Jake?" Josh said.

"Your official Halloween party host," I said.

"For real? Where?" Josh suddenly sounded wide-awake.

"Here," I said.

"What about your parents?" Josh asked.

"Off to Chicago."

"And Jessica?"

"Not a problem."

"Sweet!" Josh chuckled. "What's the plan?"

"Not sure yet," I said. "Probably just some games, punch, candy, and, mostly, no parents."

"You have to invite Amber," Josh said. "She loves to play Ghost in the Graveyard. Or we could turn your whole house into a scare house and charge admission."

"To who?" I asked.

"All the kids who come," Josh said.

"Kids don't carry money on Halloween," I said.

"UNICEF."

"No way!" I said. "That's so wrong!"

"Okay, we'll charge candy," Josh said. "One regular-size candy bar or bag to get in. None of that cheesy bite-size stuff."

"I'll think about it," I said. "Meanwhile, think about who else we want to invite. I'll call Andy."

I hung up and called Andy Kent and told him about the party. He sounded pretty enthused.

"Think about who you want to invite," I said. "We'll talk later at school."

I got off the phone and put some Pop-Tarts in the toaster for breakfast. Out of the corner of my eye I noticed Jessica standing by the doorway. She'd put on a bright yellow warm-up suit so she could go straight to the gym after school without changing.

"A party, Jake?" She arched an eyebrow. "Mom and Dad would be *so* disappointed."

"Mom and Dad aren't going to find out," I said.

"Oh?"

"Oh . . . yes," I said. "Because I'd hate to have to tell them who's been learning to drive in Kirk's car even though she still doesn't have her learner's permit."

Jessica narrowed her eyes and stabbed me with air daggers. Kirk was a friend of hers. She looked up at the kitchen clock. "It's getting late. I have to brush my teeth."

She left the kitchen and went into the small

bathroom in the front hall. It wasn't actually a whole bathroom, just a toilet, a sink, and a mirror. Mom sometimes called it a powder room. I think it was from the old days when ladies needed a place to powder their noses or something dumb like that.

"You're not supposed to use this bathroom, you know." I stopped by the door.

"You don't really expect me to go upstairs and use our bathroom." Jessica ran the water in the sink and squeezed toothpaste onto a brush.

"Why not?" I asked.

"Because it's totally gross," my sister said. "It's full of your smelly towels and your disgusting little hairs, and it reeks from that stupid deodorant you use. If I had to go in there after breakfast, I'd probably barf."

"Well, *excuuuse* me," I sputtered. "But I can't help it if my body is starting to grow extra hairs and I require deodorant. And talk about gross, look at you."

Jessica stared back at me in the mirror. "What about me?"

"Look at that toothbrush," I said. "Look how much toothpaste you put on it!"

Jessica stared down at her toothbrush. You know how most people squeeze out a line of toothpaste on their brush? My weirdo sister usually squeezed out three and sometimes *four* lines. She actually used this extra-big toothbrush just to hold that much.

"That's, like, a *mountain* of toothpaste," I said. "You could probably brush half the teeth in Jeffersonville with it. I'm amazed you can get it all into your mouth at once."

Jessica stuck her nose in the air. "So typical, Jake. You're just jealous because I have better teeth than you."

"What are you talking about?"

My sister couldn't answer because she'd started brushing her teeth and her mouth was now filled with white foam. That was another thing. She was one of the messiest teeth brushers you ever saw. It was like driving through a car wash. Big white globs of foam flying all over the place. Whenever a big glob hit the mirror, Jessica would wipe it off with some toilet paper. But that always left a white streak. And she never managed to get all the smaller spots, either.

"You think *I* leave the bathroom disgusting?" I asked. "Look at that mirror. That's the grossest thing I ever saw!"

Jessica spit out about half the foam in her mouth. "Don't exaggerate. It's just some spots."

"Just some spots?" I repeated in disbelief. "Those spots came from *your* mouth, Jessica. I mean, that's practically your spit on that mirror."

My sister actually stopped brushing for a moment and stared at the mirror as if she was seeing it for the first time through someone else's eyes. Suddenly she started brushing harder than ever! Globs of foam were flying all over the place. Even more of them splattered onto the mirror, except now she didn't even bother to wipe them away.

"What are you doing?" I asked.

"When you clean up our bathroom," Jessica said, "I'll clean up this mirror. And talk about messes. Who's going to clean up after your party?"

"Everyone."

"Oh, right." Jessica rolled her eyes in disbelief. "You really think your friends are going to hang around after the party and scrub the floors?"

"It's not a big deal," I argued. "You and I do an excellent job of messing up the house just in our normal day-to-day totally slob way of living. It's not going to take that much cleaning to go from an after-the-party mess to a Jake-and-Jessica's-normal-life mess."

Jessica ran her fingers through her short blond hair (she'd changed the color again) and thought about it. "Okay, maybe that's true. But only *if* you can keep the party under control. What happens when it gets crashed by a million kids you didn't invite?"

"It's not going to get crashed," I said.

"How do you know?"

"Because I'll make sure of it," I said.

8

Jessica pursed her lips. "Jake, can I give you my honest big-sister opinion of this scheme?"

"Why bother asking?" I shot back. "You know you're going to tell me anyway."

"You're asking for trouble," she warned.

3

"No trouble," I whispered to Amber Sweeny, Josh, and Andy an hour later at school. We were discussing the party plans.

"Amber wants Ghost in the Graveyard," Andy said. "Josh wants the scare house. I want candy corn, and you want no trouble?"

"Exactly," I said. "No trouble, as in '*This party has to be a major secret, and we have to make sure everyone we invite swears not to tell anyone else. That way no one will crash it and there'll be no trouble.*'"

"Gotcha," said Andy.

"Jake, Andy, Josh, and Amber, may I have your attention, please?" said Ms. Rogers, our social studies teacher.

"Sorry," I said. We were having social studies outside at the "farm" behind the school. It wasn't really a farm, just an area where they'd built a storage shed that served as a barn for the World's

Ugliest Cross-eyed Cow, a pig, and some ducks and chickens.

We were out there in our jackets and sweaters while Ms. Rogers gave us a "hands-on" social studies lesson in early American history.

"Can anyone tell me what kind of society is centered around farming?" Ms. Rogers asked.

Barry Dunn raised his hand. "A farming society?"

A couple of kids chuckled. Barry wrinkled his forehead and glowered at them. They instantly shut up. Barry was one of the biggest, strongest kids in the grade, and he could beat up anyone who disrespected him.

Ms. Rogers smiled patiently. "Yes, Barry, it would be a farming society, but what else could you call that?"

Julia Sax raised her hand. Julia was one of the smartest kids in our class. "An agrarian society?"

"Yes," Ms. Rogers answered with a nod. "And what would the opposite of an agrarian society be called?"

Once again Barry raised his hand. "A nonagrarian society?"

There was more chuckling. With a big grin on his face, Andy turned to Josh and me and whispered, "Did you hear that? How dumb can you —"

His voice trailed off as he realized Barry was glaring at him. "Monkey bite," Barry snarled.

My friends and I shared a puzzled look.

"Once again," Ms. Rogers said patiently, "does anyone know what else you might call it?"

"An industrial society?" asked Amber. Amber was not only one of the smartest kids in the grade but also one of the prettiest. She was tall and had blond hair and blue eyes. Every guy in the grade had a secret crush on her.

"That's correct," replied Ms. Rogers.

Meanwhile, Barry was still glaring at Andy.

"As you know, class, we've created this little farm to give you a better understanding of early America," Ms. Rogers said. "Now we're going to do some farm chores so you can get the sense of how different life was back then."

We were divided up into groups of four. And that's when things really started to go wrong.

4

The first thing that went wrong was that we got teamed up with Amanda Gluck. Amanda was a nerdy girl with thick glasses who had dedicated herself to making my friends and me miserable.

The next thing that went wrong was that we were assigned to milk the World's Ugliest Cross-eyed Cow. The World's Ugliest Cross-eyed Cow was black with large pink-and-white splotches all over her body. Her head seemed too small for the rest of her, and while her neck and ears were all black, her face was white with pale pink spots. And her eyes were permanently crossed.

Even the cows in *Far Side* cartoons didn't look as funny as she did.

"Why do we have to milk her?" Josh whined.

"Because it's your turn," Ms. Rogers answered.

"But that means we have to get close to her," I said.

"So did young men for hundreds of years," replied our social studies teacher.

"What about young women?" Andy asked, eyeing Amanda.

"I'll be glad to milk her," volunteered Amanda, who was the world's biggest brownnose.

"I'm proud of you," Ms. Rogers said.

"Great. We'll watch Amanda milk her," Josh said.

"First, you'll help Amanda get her into the shed," said Ms. Rogers.

The World's Ugliest Cross-eyed Cow was standing about twenty feet from the shed.

"Come on, you dumb cow." Josh grunted as he pulled on the thick leather strap around her neck that held her cowbell. The World's Ugliest Cross-eyed Cow had to wear a cowbell because she liked to break through the fence around the "farm" and wander off into the woods behind the school. The bell clanged when she walked, and that made it easier to find her.

No matter how hard Josh pulled, the World's Ugliest Cross-eyed Cow refused to budge.

"You have to ask her nicely," said Amanda.

"Yeah, Josh." Andy grinned. "Say please."

"She's a cow," Josh grumbled. "She doesn't understand please."

"Then say moo," I said.

"Or moooove," said Andy.

"Good one!" Andy and I shared a high five.

Meanwhile, Josh hadn't gotten the World's Ugliest Cross-eyed Cow to budge an inch.

Andy bent forward and looked closely at the World's Ugliest Cross-eyed Cow's nose. "Wow, check out the size of those nostrils."

I looked closer. "They're way huge!"

"Hairy, too," Andy observed.

"Way hairy," I agreed.

"Kind of wet," said Andy.

As if the World's Ugliest Cross-eyed Cow had heard him, she stuck out her long pink tongue and licked her nose.

"Gross!" Andy jumped back.

"Way gross!" I agreed.

"You guys want to help instead of fooling around?" Josh grumbled. Andy and I took hold of the leather strap around the World's Ugliest Cross-eyed Cow's neck.

"One, two, three!" Josh counted.

We pulled as hard as we could. The World's Ugliest Cross-eyed Cow didn't budge.

"Either we're totally weak, or this cow is incredibly strong." Andy grimaced as we pulled with all our might.

"Incredibly heavy is more like it," Josh mumbled, and let go of the leather strap. "Forget it. I give up."

Andy and I let go, too.

"You guys just don't understand her." Amanda gently stroked the cow's snout.

"And you do?" I asked.

"Better than you," Amanda said.

"Yeah, right," Josh scoffed.

"Want to bet I can get her into the shed?" Amanda asked.

"Sure," said Andy. "Just name it."

Amanda leaned close and whispered, "I get to come to your party tomorrow night."

I blinked in shock. "How do you know about that?" I whispered.

"I heard you talking to Amber," Amanda said.

"Uh, excuse us for a second." I pulled my friends into a huddle.

"What do we do?" I whispered.

"Tell her she can't come," said Josh.

"You do that and she'll tell the whole school about the party," Andy pointed out.

"I guess that settles it." I sighed and turned back to Amanda. "Okay, here's the deal. If you can get the cow into the shed, you can come to the party. But you have to keep it a secret."

"Deal." Amanda turned to the World's Ugliest Cross-eyed Cow.

"Don't sweat it, dudes," Josh whispered. "There's no way she's going to get that thing to move."

5

Amanda stroked the cow's pink spotted snout. "Come on, sweetness. Don't you want to get milked? I bet you'll feel a lot better once you've had your udder emptied."

My friends and I watched in amazement as the World's Ugliest Cross-eyed Cow started to follow Amanda into the storage shed.

"How'd she do that?" I asked.

"I guess she relates to cows," Andy said.

"A lot better than she relates to people," Josh pointed out.

"It just so happens that cows are a lot smarter than people give them credit for," Amanda said.

"Like you, right?" Josh asked

"You're so not funny," Amanda snapped.

"I bet you didn't know that cows cause pollution," said Andy.

"It happens to be part of their natural digestive process," Amanda replied. "They emit methane gas."

"Emit it how?" I asked.

"The same way people do, dummy," said Josh.

Andy frowned for a moment. Then his eyes went wide. "You mean, when you look at a bunch of cows in a field, they're all *emitting* gas?"

"All animals emit gas," Amanda said.

"She's right," I said. "Even Lance *emits* once in a while. And when he does, look out."

"Yeah, but a whole field of cows all emitting at once," Andy said. "I mean, that's cow power!"

Ms. Rogers came over. "I thought you boys were going to get the cow into the shed."

"We couldn't do it," Josh said.

"Amanda doesn't seem to be having a problem," Ms. Rogers said.

"Amanda understands cows," Andy said.

Inside the shed, Ms. Rogers put a bucket under the World's Ugliest Cross-eyed Cow's udder and pulled up a stool. Then she turned to us. "Ready, Josh?"

Josh's face fell. "I thought Amanda was going to milk her."

"Since Amanda got the cow into the shed, I think you should," said our teacher.

"Don't forget, Josh," I teased, "it's part of the early American experience."

"So is hunting buffalo with a bow and arrow," Josh muttered. "How come we're not doing that?"

"Maybe because there are no buffaloes around here," Andy said.

"So? We could hunt the World's Ugliest Cross-eyed Cow instead," Josh said.

"That wouldn't be fun," I said. "She'd just stand here and wait for us."

"She could fight back with cow-power emissions," Andy said.

"You think that's why they used bows and arrows?" Josh realized. "So they wouldn't have to get close enough to smell the emissions!"

"Enough talking, Josh." Ms. Rogers nodded down at the stool. "Get to work."

Josh sat down on the stool. "Now what?"

"Take one teat in each hand and squeeze from the top down," Ms. Rogers instructed. "You want to squeeze her milk out of the bottom of the teat and into the bucket."

Josh started to milk. The World's Ugliest Cross-eyed Cow moved her mouth as if she was chewing.

"What's she chewing?" Andy asked.

"Her cud," answered Amanda.

"What's cud?" Andy asked.

"Her food."

Andy looked around. "I don't see any food."

"She ate it before and held it in her stomach," Amanda explained. "Now she has time to bring it back up and chew it."

Andy's jaw dropped. "You mean she kind of barfed it back into her mouth to chew it some more?"

"Sort of."

Andy stared at the World's Ugliest Cross-eyed Cow in awe. "This thing is amazing! It's ugly, it licks its own nose, gives off cow-power emissions, and chews on its own barf. Talk about a new standard for gross."

"Ladies and gentlemen, introducing the World's Ugliest Cross-eyed Cow," I announced. "Now setting a new standard for gross, and sponsored by the Cudweiser Chewing Company. Remember, folks, this Cud's for you!"

Ms. Rogers smiled. "That's funny, Jake."

"Thank you." I bowed.

"Know what else is funny?" Josh said from the stool. "I can't get any milk out of this thing."

"Are you squeezing from the top down?" Ms. Rogers asked.

"I think so," Josh said.

"Let me try." Ms. Rogers replaced Josh on the stool and started to milk the World's Ugliest Cross-eyed Cow. Meanwhile, Andy tapped Josh and me on the shoulder and nodded over at Barry, who was tossing feed from a bucket to the chickens.

When Barry saw us, he bent his fingers like a claw and slowly opened and closed them. "Monkey bite," he growled.

"Would someone please tell me what a monkey bite is?" Andy whispered.

"I don't know," I whispered back.

"Neither do I," said Josh. "But I have a feeling that before the day is over Andy's going to find out."

6

After social studies, we headed to the boys' room. Luckily for Andy, there was no sign of Barry anywhere. My friends and I each stood at a sink and scrubbed all traces of the World's Ugliest Cross-eyed Cow off our hands.

"Am I glad that's over," I said, relieved.

"Now we can get back to the main mission," said Josh. "Inviting kids to the party."

"We have to be really careful," I cautioned them. "We've already got Amanda coming. I don't want anyone else to find out except the kids we want to be there. Otherwise, it's going to be a zoo. Right, Andy?"

Andy didn't answer. He was standing at the sink. The water was running, but he wasn't washing his hands. In fact, he wasn't moving at all.

"I just remembered something!" he gasped. "I have an extra credit project due tomorrow."

"What for?" I asked.

"To make up for a test I totally bombed in English. Since Halloween is coming, Ms. Bunson said I could do a report on vampires. Only I forgot."

"Chill, dude," I said. "You've still got tonight."

"You expect me to do *a whole report* tonight?" Andy winced at the thought. "When would I have time to watch TV?"

"Don't wait until tonight," I said as I rinsed my hands. "You can start right now. What else are you going to do today?"

"Go to classes," Andy said.

"What do you do in class, Andy?" Josh asked.

"I don't know," Andy answered. "Doodle and daydream and get into trouble. Stuff like that."

"Then it's perfect," I said. "Just for today, think of all those classes as time to do your schoolwork."

"Whoa! You're right!" Andy cried. "I could do schoolwork in class. I never thought of that!"

"And then you'll still have time to watch TV tonight," I said. "Why don't you go to the library right now and get on the Internet and see what they have on vampires?"

Andy started to dry his hands. "Great idea! Thanks for the suggestion, Jake. Catch you guys at lunch." He hurried out of the boys' room.

"Imagine that," Josh chuckled. "Andy doing

schoolwork in school. Like it's some totally new idea he'd never thought of before."

"Yeah." I nodded.

Josh shook his head. "Sometimes that kid really scares me."

7

Josh and I spent the rest of the morning inviting our friends to the party. We told each of them that it had to be a total secret. By lunchtime we'd invited everyone.

"You asked Alex Silver and Howie Jamison?" Josh asked as we came out of the lunch line with our trays.

"And Ollie Hawkins," I said. "I know he's only in sixth grade, but he's a good kid. Did you tell Amber and Julia?"

"Roger that," Josh said. "And Mica Channing."

Mica was another really cute girl.

"There's just one problem," Josh added. "Mica and Amber both really want it to be a costume party."

"Costumes?" I grimaced. "No way."

"It doesn't have to be that bad," Josh said. "You and I can wear normal clothes and pretend we're dressed up as teenagers. Andy can wear

25

normal clothes and pretend he's the village idiot."

I grinned as we sat down at our regular table. "Where's Andy anyway?"

"Probably in the library working on his report," Josh said.

"Andy skipped lunch to do schoolwork?" I chuckled. "That's a first."

The words were hardly out of my mouth when Andy appeared.

"Speak of the devil," Josh said.

"Speak of the vampire," Andy replied as he put his tray down on the table.

"How's the report coming?" I asked.

"What kind of dog does Dracula own?" Andy asked.

"I don't know," I said.

"A bloodhound," said Andy. "Why did the vampire need mouthwash?"

"Why?"

"He had bat breath. Where does a vampire eat lunch?"

"I thought you were doing a report," I said.

"I am," said Andy.

"Then how come you're telling us vampire jokes?" asked Josh.

"Because I found this really mad cool Web site," Andy said. "Now come on, you haven't said where a vampire eats lunch."

"Where?" asked Josh.

"In a casketeria!" Andy announced. "Is that funny or what?"

"It's funny, Andy," I said. "But what have you learned about vampires?"

"Where does Dracula water-ski?" Andy asked.

"Stop telling us vampire jokes," I said. "Tell us what you're going to put in your report."

"Vampire stuff," he said.

"Like what?" Josh asked.

"I don't know." Andy shrugged. "I haven't gotten to it yet."

"You spent the whole morning looking at vampire jokes on the Internet?" I asked.

"Hey, you have to admit they're pretty funny," Andy said defensively.

I couldn't help smirking. "I don't think Ms. Bunson's going to give you credit for vampire jokes."

Andy's shoulders slumped. "It would be a funny report."

"Didn't you learn *anything* about vampires this morning?" Josh asked.

"Absolutely." Andy sat up. "I learned that Dracula likes to water-ski on Lake Erie. Like eerie. Get it?"

"Yeah, we get it," I groaned.

"And *you're* gonna get an F if you give her a report that's all jokes," Josh said.

I glanced up at the cafetorium clock. "You've

got two periods left, Andy. How are you going to get that report done?"

"Uh, with your help?" Andy guessed.

Josh and I looked at each other and sighed. It was probably the only way.

8

That afternoon we stayed late in the library and helped Andy finish his vampire report. I hate to admit it, but it was actually kind of interesting.

"Know what's amazing?" I asked as we left the library.

Josh pointed out the windows. "That we actually stayed in school until it was almost dark?"

"Well, there's that," I allowed. "But also how many different cultures had myths about vampires. They had them in Europe and Africa and Asia for centuries. Isn't it weird? I mean, how could they all know about vampires?"

"Maybe they're not myths," Andy said. "Maybe they're real."

"Boys?" someone called. We turned and saw Ms. Rogers wearing a tan suede jacket and hurrying down the hall toward us. "Am I glad I ran into you three. Could you please do me a huge favor? The cow got loose again, and I'm late for a doctor's appointment. Could you go get her and put her back in the shed?"

Josh had a pained look on his face.

"It shouldn't be hard to find her," Ms. Rogers went on. "Just follow the sound of her bell."

"Finding her isn't what I'm worried about," Josh replied. "It's getting her back into the shed."

"Just talk nicely to her," Ms. Rogers advised. "Remember, she may not know what you're saying, but she'll respond to the tone of your voice."

"We'll be glad to do it," I said. Andy and I took Josh by the arms and led him away.

"Thank you so much!" Ms. Rogers rushed toward the doors.

"You're turning into a worse brownnose than Amanda," Josh grumbled when the teacher was out of earshot.

"Ms. Rogers is really nice and she needs help," I said as we headed down the hall and toward the back of the school. "There's nothing wrong with helping someone. Even a teacher."

"And you heard what she said about the World's Ugliest Cross-eyed Cow," said Andy. "All we have to do is be polite."

We let ourselves out through the doors at the back of the science wing. Behind the school were the athletic fields, and beyond them were the woods where we knew we'd find the World's Ugliest Cross-eyed Cow.

We started across the grassy football field. The

sun was setting, and the last long shadows of the day were gradually fading to gray. Ahead of us loomed the ever-darkening woods.

"How come we don't hear the bell?" Andy asked.

"Depends on how deep into the woods she went," I guessed.

"The bell only rings when the World's Ugliest Cross-eyed Cow moves," Josh said. "What if she's just standing around?"

"Why would she just stand around?" I asked.

"Because she's a cow, dummy," Josh said. "All they ever do is stand around."

"And emit cow-power emissions," Andy added.

"She's probably standing in the woods without a clue what to do next," Josh said.

"Then how are we going to find her?" Andy asked.

"We'll call her," I said.

"Yeah." Josh smiled. "We'll call her really nicely. Like, 'Come here, Miss World's Ugliest Cross-eyed Cow, please?' "

By now we'd crossed the football field. All that separated us from the woods was a thin strip of tall grass and weeds. The woods looked dark. My friends and I stopped.

Andy bit his lip. "How do we know the World's Ugliest Cross-eyed Cow is even in there?"

"Because that's where she usually goes when she gets loose," I said.

"What if she went someplace else?" Andy asked.

"Like where?" Josh asked.

"I don't know, the mall or Burger King or something," Andy said.

"Right," Josh scoffed, "she went to Burger King so she could see what she's gonna look like as a hamburger."

"Might be an improvement," I said. "After all, she *is* the World's Ugliest Cross-eyed Cow."

"Look, we all know exactly where she is." Josh pointed into the dark woods. "She's in *there*. And you're the brave guys who told Ms. Rogers we'd go get her. And the longer we wait, the colder and darker it's going to get, so let's go already."

Andy and I stared into the woods. All we could see were dark tree trunks, branches with a few dead brown leaves, and shadows.

"What's wrong with you chickens?" Josh asked. "It's just the woods. We've been in there a million times."

"Not on the night before Halloween," said Andy.

"What difference does that make?" Josh asked.

Ahhhhhwoooooooooooooo! A ghostly howl suddenly came from the woods.

9

Josh must have jumped five feet. "What was *that*?!"

"Sounded like a wolf." Andy's voice quivered.

"What's wrong with you?" I said. "There are no wolves around here."

"Then what was it?" Andy asked.

"Probably a dog," I said.

"Didn't sound like a dog," Josh said.

"Well, it couldn't be a wolf," I said.

"Maybe it was a fox," said Andy.

"That's not what a fox sounds like," Josh said.

"How do you know what a fox sounds like?" I asked.

"Foxes don't howl," Josh insisted.

"What do they do?" Andy asked.

"I don't know," Josh said. "Maybe they sing. What difference does it make?"

"I still say it was a wolf," said Andy.

Clang! From somewhere in the woods came the sound of the cowbell.

"Did you hear that?" I asked. "It's the cow, and she doesn't sound that far away. Come on."

I took a few steps into the tall grass at the edge of the woods. Just as I reached the trees something big flew out, flapping its wings loudly as it flew over my head.

"Whoa!" I ducked. "What was *that?*"

"A bat!" Andy cried.

"No way, it was too big," I said.

"Looked like a bat to me," said Josh.

"Forget it," I insisted. "I've seen bats before. They're, like, the size of sparrows. Or maybe a tiny bit bigger. That thing was the size of a goose. A *big* goose."

"Maybe it was a bat goose," said Josh.

"Or a goose bat," suggested Andy.

"Come on, guys," I said. "Let's just go get the cow. Otherwise we're going to stand around and talk all night."

Josh and Andy looked at each other.

"I say we stand around and talk," said Andy.

"Sounds good to me," said Josh.

"What about the cow?" I asked.

"You get the cow," Josh said. "We'll stay here and listen to the foxes howl."

"And we'll count the goose bats that come flying out," added Andy.

"You guys are total chickens," I said.

Josh put his hands in his armpits and flapped

his elbows up and down like wings. "Bawk, bawk, bawk!"

Ahhhhhwoooooooooooooo! Another ghostly howl came from the woods.

"That is definitely a wolf," Andy said with a trembling voice.

"Here's an idea," Josh said. "Maybe, if we talk nice, we can get the cow to come to us, instead of us going to the cow."

The three of us stood at the edge of the woods and started to call.

"Yoo-hoo! World's Most Beautiful Cow, please come out," Andy called.

"We love you, and we'd really like to see you," called Josh.

"And we're sorry if we ever said anything not nice to you," I added.

Clang! Clang! The cowbell rang.

"She's coming!" Andy cried.

"Amazing!" said Josh.

"Come on, World's Most Beautiful Cow, you can do it!" Andy yelled.

"You are the best!" cried Josh.

Clang! Clang! The cow's pale face appeared through the dark tree trunks.

"That's it!" Andy said. "What a good little cow you are!"

It wasn't long before the World's Ugliest Cross-eyed Cow lumbered out of the woods. My friends and I spoke softly to her as we led her back to the shed and locked her inside.

Ahhhhhwoooooooooooooo! No sooner had we gotten her safely into the shed than another howl drifted across the athletic fields toward us.

"Come on, guys, let's go home," said Andy. "This is totally freaky."

"No way I'm walking around out here in the dark," Josh said. "Let's cut through school."

"We're not supposed to," Andy said.

"It's not a big deal," Josh said. "The lights are still on."

Even though it was nearly dinnertime and the school was empty, the classrooms were brightly lit.

"What's going on?" Andy asked.

"Maybe there's a meeting or something," Josh speculated.

"No, look." I pointed through the doors at the end of the science wing. Inside we could see a tall, thin man in a green uniform mopping the hallway. "It's the custodian."

"That's weird," said Andy. "I never saw him before."

"Who cares?" said Josh. "We're just cutting through school. He won't mind."

We went through the doors at the back of the science wing. But inside, the floor was wet. My friends and I stopped on the big black rubber mat just inside the doors. Ahead of us, the long hallway glistened with a thin coat of water.

The custodian stared down at the floor as he mopped from an old gray metal bucket on wheels. He was using an old-fashioned mop with a bunch of knotted gray strings at the end. Each time he pushed the bucket, the wheels would squeak loudly. He was tall and very pale. I couldn't get a good look at his face, but like Andy, I was pretty sure I'd never seen him before. There was definitely something creepy about the way he kept his head bowed, as if he didn't want us to see him.

"Come on, let's go," Josh said.

"We can't," I said. "The floor's all wet. We'll leave footsteps."

You know how sometimes you talk a little extra loud because you want someone to hear? I think we were hoping the custodian would tell us it was okay to make tracks in the wet hall. But he just kept mopping.

"Maybe we ought to wait," Andy said.

"But I'm going to be late for dinner," Josh complained.

"It von't take long," the custodian mumbled in a deep voice and a strange accent.

My friends and I shared a nervous look.

"So, uh, I guess we should just wait, right?" I asked.

"Yah." The custodian finished mopping and left

the old mop in the bucket of dirty gray water. He pulled the bucket onto the rubber mat where we were standing. My friends and I pressed our backs against the wall opposite him. His head was still bowed. He had black hair that fell into his eyes. The skin on his hands and face was so pale it was almost gray.

My friends and I glanced anxiously at the wet floor, praying it would dry quickly so we could get out of there.

The custodian stared down at the black rubber mat and said nothing. The silence was spooky.

"Ahem," Andy cleared his throat. "I thought the school had a new machine for cleaning the floors. How come you use that old mop and bucket?"

The custodian slowly raised his head. He had dark eyes and a long, thin nose, and his upper lip had two slight bulges near the corners of his mouth.

"Zis is how I learn to do it in zee old country," he answered in a deep monotone.

"How come we've never seen you around school before?" I asked.

"I vork nights," the custodian replied, and sadly gazed out into the dark.

"So, uh, what's your name?" Andy asked.

"I am Vlad," he said.

"V-V-Vlad?" Andy repeated in a trembling voice.

"Vlad, huh?" Josh grinned. "Well, I'm vlad to meet you."

Vlad the custodian grinned slightly. As his upper lip rose over his teeth, I saw what caused those bulges. His two upper teeth at the front corners were longer than the others. In fact, they almost looked like fangs.

10

Luckily, the floor had dried enough for Vlad to let us go. As my friends and I hurried down the hall, Andy kept looking back over his shoulder at the creepy custodian.

"What's with you?" Josh asked.

"I'll tell you later," Andy whispered.

We cut through school and went out the front doors and into the dark.

"That was weird," Andy said as we headed away from Burt Ipchupt Middle School. "Just totally weird."

"He was kind of strange," I agreed.

"Way past strange," Andy said. "Did you see his skin? His teeth? Did you hear his name?"

"Yeah, Vlad," said Josh.

"Like Vlad the Impaler!" Andy exclaimed. "The dude who started the whole vampire thing. He was supposed to be the original Count Dracula."

"Why'd they call him the Impaler?" I asked as we turned down a dark, tree-lined street.

"Because he was one sick dude," Andy said. "He used to kill his enemies by dropping them on sharpened poles sticking out of the ground."

"Crude, but effective," I said. "But you really don't think that Vlad the custodian is a vampire."

"I'm saying it's a serious possibility," Andy said. "He's got the name, the pale skin, the pointy teeth, and he works nights."

"Can we stop talking about this?" Josh asked.

"Why?" I asked back.

"Because we're walking down a dark street on the night before Halloween and it's all getting a little too creepy for me," Josh said.

"Come off it, Josh," I said. "Nothing's going to happen here."

The words had hardly left my mouth when a group of kids came around the corner. They were lit up for a moment by a lone streetlight. It was Barry Dunn and his buddies, and they were coming our way!

11

My friends and I ducked behind some bushes. If Barry was dangerous *in* school, that was nothing compared to the way he was *outside* of school where teachers couldn't catch him.

Josh, Andy, and I stayed low and held our breaths as Barry and his buddies passed.

"The great thing about the monkey bite is it really kills, but it doesn't leave a mark," Barry was saying. "A kid can go to a teacher, but he won't have any proof that you touched him."

"You gotta show us how to do it," begged one of his buddies.

"I will," Barry promised. "As soon as I get my hands on Andy Kent."

Even after Barry passed, my friends and I stayed behind the bushes. We wanted to make sure Barry and his buddies were long gone. When we finally came out, Andy looked pale and scared.

"I hate to say this," Josh said as we started walking again, "but it sounds bad."

"What are you going to do?" I asked.

Andy made a determined fist. "Fight back."

"Against Barry *and* his buddies?" Josh sounded surprised.

"Roger that, amigo."

"Then I have one last question," said Josh. "After Barry kills you, can I have your CD burner?"

12

The next morning, after my parents left for Chicago, I joined my friends and walked to school. Andy was carrying a big Super Soaker water gun with bright green and orange plastic water tanks. He was wearing a bunch of small roundish white things around his neck.

"What's that?"

"Garlic," he said. "It keeps vampires away."

"Are you for real?"

Andy reached inside his shirt and pulled out a small wooden cross on a string.

"More protection?" Josh guessed.

"If I were you, I'd be more worried about Barry than vampires," I said.

"That's what the water gun's for," said Andy.

"Right." Josh smirked. "That'll stop him."

"You bring that thing into school and you'll get in way big trouble," I warned him.

"Not if I need it for a science project," Andy said.

"I thought you said it was for Barry."

"It is." Andy wasn't making sense. Even worse, that garlic around his neck looked ridiculous.

"You wear that garlic into school and everyone's gonna think you're whacked," I said.

"Better that than joining the ranks of the undead," Andy answered solemnly.

13

Andy's answer sounded weird, but I didn't have much time to think about it because as soon as we stepped through the school doors Richie Greedlick came up to us. Richie's dad, Stanley, owned the Maximum Pro-Fit Sports store at the mall.

"Yo, Jake, that's so cool that you're having a party tonight," he said. "I'll see you there."

No sooner did he leave than Debbie Sloane came up. Debbie's older sister, Stacy, was in Jessica's grade at the high school. "I can't believe you're having an open house Halloween party. Everyone's totally psyched."

"Everyone?" I swallowed.

It was true. I could hardly take a step down the hall without someone mentioning the party. Andy went into Mr. Dirksen's science lab to stash the Super Soaker. Josh and I waited for him.

"How'd everyone find out?" Josh asked me.

"Someone must have blabbed," I said. "Any guesses?"

Josh didn't answer. He was staring at something past me. "Uh-oh."

I turned and found myself face-to-face with Barry Dunn.

"Where's Andy?" he asked.

"Uh, I don't know," I answered, praying Andy wouldn't come out of the science lab.

"Heard you're having a party tonight," Barry said.

"Oh?" I replied nervously.

"Don't act like you don't know what I'm talking about," Barry snarled. "Me and my friends will be there. You supply the treats. We'll bring the tricks."

This was starting to sound really bad. First, practically every kid in school knew about the party, and now Barry said he was crashing. Barry and his buddies left.

"What are we going to do?" Josh asked.

"There's only one thing we can do," I replied sadly. "Cancel the party."

14

Andy jogged out of the science room just as I said we had to cancel the party.

"Are you for real?" He skidded to a stop.

"Yes," I said.

Andy turned to Josh. "What do you think?"

"I think Amber's coming this way, and she looks really happy," said Josh.

He was right. Amber Sweeny, who was tall, beautiful, blond, and smart, was skipping toward us with a smile on her lips and a sparkle in her eyes.

"I'm so excited, Jake," she gushed. "I just love Halloween parties. And costume parties are my favorite. And I hear we're going to play Ghost in the Graveyard."

"Uh —" I wanted to tell Amber that the party was canceled, but suddenly it wasn't so easy.

"Will you be my partner?" Amber asked.

"Partner?" I repeated.

"We'll hide together in the dark and scare people," Amber said.

Josh and Andy started to grin. *Hide in the dark with Amber?* It was every guy's secret wish.

"Jake, you are so cool for doing this," Amber said. "I can't wait. See you later."

Amber skipped down the hall to her next class.

"Still want to cancel the party?" Andy asked.

"Guess not." I shrugged.

"There he is!" Barry burst through the crowd of kids in the hall in front of us. His buddies were right behind him.

"Hey, Andy!" Barry shouted gleefully. "It's monkey bite time!"

My friends and I ran. We turned a corner and skidded to a stop, looking around for a classroom to hide in.

"Here!" Josh pointed at a door with big red letters: JANITOR'S CLOSET. KEEP OUT.

"Forget it," I said. "It's always locked."

"Not today." Josh pushed on the door, and it started to open.

"But it says keep out," Andy said.

"Exactly," said Josh. "Which is why Barry'll never look in it. Come on!"

We piled into the closet and closed the door behind us. It was dark inside. The air felt damp and smelled sour, like an old, mildewed mop. Josh pressed his ear against the door. I stood behind him, and Andy was behind me. The loudest sound was the three of us breathing hard after running.

"Uh, guys?" Andy whispered.

"*Shhh!*" Josh hushed him. "*You want Barry to hear us?*"

"No, but —"

"*Then keep quiet!*"

Out in the hall we could hear the slap of footsteps approaching. My heart was pounding. Half from running and half from fear.

We heard Barry say, "Where'd they go?" and one of his friends said, "They must be around here somewhere."

Andy tapped me on the back again.

"*Not now, Andy.*"

Out in the hall someone said, "What about the janitor's closet?"

My heart started to pound twice as hard. Again I felt someone tap me on the back.

"*Not now!*" I hissed.

"*But you have to see this!*" Andy hissed back.

Not knowing any other way to keep him quiet, I turned. Andy pointed at something on the floor behind him. Now that my eyes had adjusted to the dark, it was no longer pitch-black in the janitor's closet. A tiny bit of light slipped in under the door. Just enough to help me see the vague outline of the thing Andy was pointing at.

It looked exactly like . . . a casket!

"Ah!" The yelp escaped my lips before I could stop it.

Josh spun around. "What?"

I pointed a trembling finger at the casket. Suddenly we heard a creaking sound, like a hinge turning. But it wasn't the hinge on the closet door. It was the hinge on the casket as the top began to rise!

"AHHHHHHHHHH!!!!!" My friends and I screamed and burst out of the janitor's closet.

Out in the hall, Barry and his buddies spun around. A nasty smile appeared on Barry's face when he saw Andy. He cracked his knuckles. "Welcome to Monkey Bite Land."

15

Josh and I managed to escape. Andy was the only one Barry wanted. We had an agreement that whenever Barry and his buddies nailed one of us, the other guys were under no obligation to do anything heroic that might lead to them getting tortured, too.

In science class that day, we had a free period where we could fool around and experiment with stuff. It was exactly the kind of thing Mr. Dirksen had never allowed before he and I switched bodies. But ever since then, Mr. Dirksen had become a much cooler teacher. It hadn't hurt that he'd married Ms. Rogers, either. That seemed to make him happier, too.

Josh and I were fooling around with a supersaturated solution that was supposed to grow blue crystals when Andy came in with a big frown on his face. He went to the back of the room where the DITS was covered by a blue plastic tarp. The DITS, or Dirksen Intelligence Transfer System, was a machine the "old" Mr. Dirksen had invented to help students learn without teachers having to teach. But it had never worked correctly. Instead, it usually made people switch bodies, as I had with various teachers, a movie star, an alien, my dog, Lance, and the President of the United States.

The other thing the DITS could do, when reconfigured in a different way, was shrink people's heads. When it did that, it was called the DUNCE, or Dirksen Unique Negating Cranium Effector.

But now, under the blue tarp, the DITS/DUNCE was in a state of disrepair. Various parts had been removed, and a lot of wires and cables lay on the floor around it. Andy lifted a corner of the tarp.

"What happened in Monkey Bite Land?" I asked.

"I got monkey bit, what else?" Andy muttered unhappily.

"How'd they do it?" Josh asked.

"One guy holds you down while the other two give you the claw between your neck and your shoulder and just above your knee."

The thought of it made me wince.

"Must have hurt, huh?" Josh said.

Andy nodded and stared at the DITS/DUNCE. "You think we could ever get this thing to work again?"

"The DITS? I hope not." Every time I got involved with the DITS it turned into big trouble. Although our most recent stunt, when we switched bodies with professional wrestlers, had been pretty funny.

"I was thinking more of the DUNCE," Andy said. "Like Barry getting his head shrunk for Halloween."

"Forget it." I pointed at all the wires on the floor around the DITS/DUNCE. "This thing is fried."

"Maybe." Andy let the tarp fall and went back to a table where his Super Soaker lay in pieces. I noticed a couple of cans of shaving cream on the table, too.

"I'm doing a conversion," Andy said. "From Super Soaker to Super Creamer."

"As in shaving cream?" Josh asked.

"You got it." Andy picked up the Super Creamer and pretended to aim it. Instead of the little squirt hole at the end of the barrel, there was now a wider opening.

"Range?" I asked.

"With three fully charged cans it should reach twenty-five or thirty feet," Andy answered.

"Coverage?" I asked.

"Total saturation in eight to ten seconds."

"Accuracy?"

"Probably its weakest feature," Andy admitted. "Let's just say the closer, the better. I think Barry'll like it."

"When you shoot him with it?" I asked.

"No, when I give it to him as a present."

Josh and I stared at him, completely puzzled.

"You're joking, right?" I said.

Clang! An unexpected sound came from the hall outside the science lab.

"What was that?" Alex Silver asked.

"The cowbell," said Josh.

"Inside school?" said Julia Sax.

Clang! It sounded like it was coming closer. Mr. Dirksen went over and opened the science room door.

Clang! Clop! Clop! Clang! With the door open there was no doubt about what we heard. The cowbell and the clopping of hoofs on the tile floor. Up and down the hall, doors were opening and kids were sticking their heads out as the World's Ugliest Cross-eyed Cow came to school.

"Maybe she wants an education," joked Julia.

"I think she came to see me," announced Amanda Gluck.

A lot of kids snickered, but the weird thing was the World's Ugliest Cross-eyed Cow went right up to Amanda.

"Aw, true love," laughed Alex Silver.

Amanda wrinkled her nose. "You're just jealous."

"Right," Alex chuckled. "I'm jealous of a cow."

Amanda ignored him and stroked the cow's snout. "It was nice of you to come see me, sweetness, but you're not supposed to be in school. Come on, let's go back where you belong."

Clang! Clop! Clop! Clang! We watched in amazement as the World's Ugliest Cross-eyed Cow turned around and followed Amanda back down the hall toward the doors.

"Amanda's finally found someone who understands her," Josh said.

Everyone went back into the classrooms and soon forgot that the World's Ugliest Cross-eyed Cow wanted an education. As soon as school ended my friends and I headed for the supermarket and the party store to get food and decorations. Then, loaded down with the shopping bags, we walked to my house. Almost all the houses on our block were decorated with jack-o'-lanterns and scarecrows and witches on brooms and fake spiderwebs.

"This reminds me," I said. "What was the story with that casket in the janitor's closet?"

"That's right!" Andy gasped. "I totally forgot! That proves Vlad's a vampire!"

"No, it doesn't," Josh said. "It just proves there's some kind of tool chest in there."

"Why can't you admit that Vlad's a vampire?" Andy asked as we went into my house. Lance was asleep in the front hall. He got up and sniffed Josh and Andy for a second. But he knew them and soon yawned and lay down again.

"Because there's no such thing as a vampire," Josh said. "And even if there was, why would he work as a custodian?"

"Maybe it pays well," Andy said.

Josh shook his head. "You can't be *that* stupid."

It was starting to get dark, and we were nowhere near ready to have a party. We went into the kitchen and started to unpack the grocery bags. Outside on the sidewalk we could see groups of little kids in costumes being led around by adults. Then the doorbell rang, and Lance started to bark.

"Trick-or-treaters," I said. "I better go get it."

"I'll do it," Andy said. "I need to run home and get into my costume anyway."

"Okay," I said. "Leave the bowl of candy outside the front door so anyone who comes by can help themselves."

"Gotcha." Andy left. Josh and I got back to work. We set up the refreshment table in the backyard and put up Halloween decorations. It was dark by the time we finished. The first of our friends started to arrive. Alex Silver showed up wearing a cowboy hat with a fake arrow going through it. Mica Channing came dressed as Laura Croft, the computer figure, in yellow-and-green tights.

I checked my watch. Andy had been gone for a long time.

"Has anyone seen Andy?" I asked.

"I just saw him going back to school," Mica said.

Josh and I shared a puzzled look, as if we were both thinking, *Why in the world would Andy go back to school on Halloween night?*

Then I remembered something. I pulled Josh off to the side and whispered, "This morning he was talking about shrinking Barry's head."

"Good," Josh whispered back.

"No, *not* good," I said. "The DITS is a mess. If Andy tries to use it, Barry could get seriously hurt."

Josh pursed his lips. "So?"

"I mean, *really* hurt," I whispered. "As much as he deserves it, it's not right."

Josh nodded reluctantly. "Okay, so what do we do?"

"We better go to school," I said.

16

I told Mica and Alex to keep the party going and that Josh and I would be back as fast as possible.

"I can't believe we left our own party to save Barry," Josh complained as we jogged along the dark sidewalk. We turned a corner . . . and skidded to a stop. Barry and his friends were coming down the sidewalk toward us. They were carrying backpacks.

"Hey, look who's here," Barry said with a nasty smile.

"Gee, Barry, it's funny to see you with a backpack on," I said. "You never wear one to school."

"This one ain't filled with books," Barry said.

"I never would have guessed," Josh quipped.

"Listen, Barry, you wouldn't mind telling us where you're going, would you?" I asked.

Barry squinted suspiciously. "Maybe I would."

"To school to meet Andy?" Josh asked.

"How'd you know?" said Barry.

"Don't do it," I warned.

"Why?" Barry asked.

"Just don't," Josh said. Neither of us wanted to tell him that Andy was setting a trap, because that would just make Barry want to monkey bite Andy some more.

"But he promised me something," Barry said.

"The Super Creamer gun?" Josh guessed.

Barry nodded. "We made a deal. He gives me the Super Creamer, and I won't pick on him anymore."

"Suppose Josh and I go to school and get it for you?" I said.

"Why?" Barry asked.

"You have to take our word," I said. "It's the best thing."

Barry made a face. "Do I look that stupid?"

Josh and I shared a quick glance. It was tempting to answer, but we knew it would mean maximum monkey bite torture.

"Give us half an hour," I said. "If we're not back here with the Super Creamer, you can go to school and get it."

"Fifteen minutes," Barry countered.

"Twenty minutes," I said.

"Deal," Barry said. "But if this is a trick, it won't just be a monkey bite for you two. It'll be the monkey bite gorilla slam."

17

"**W**hat's a gorilla slam?" Josh asked as we hurried up the dark front walk to school.

"I don't want to find out," I answered as I tried the front doors. "Darn, they're locked."

"School looks really dark," Josh said. "I guess Vlad's out trick-or-treating."

"Let's go around the back," I said.

We jogged around to the back of the school. Once again, the lights were on in the science wing. Josh and I went to the doors. Someone, probably Andy, had wedged a piece of cardboard into the doorway to stop the doors from locking.

Josh hesitated. "If we get caught in school on Halloween night, we're going to be in totally huge trouble. More than normal trouble, because they're going to think we came to school to do something bad."

"All we're going to do is find Andy and get out of here," I assured him.

We tiptoed down the hall to Mr. Dirksen's room and slowly pushed open the door.

Inside, the lights were on. At first we didn't see anyone. Then we heard tinkering sounds over by the DITS. Andy was under the blue tarp, splicing together some wires.

"Forget about it, Andy," I said. "Barry's not coming."

Andy looked up with wide, surprised eyes. "Wha'?"

"We figured out what you were up to and told him not to come," Josh said.

"Why?" Andy asked, upset.

"Because you can't go around shrinking people's heads," I said.

"Then how come it's okay for him to give us monkey bites?" Andy shot back.

"It's not," I said. "But two wrongs don't make a right."

"Well, it sure would make me feel better to see him with a head the size of a softball," Andy argued.

"Frankly, he's not far from that size now," Josh said. "I'd go for something around the size of a tennis ball."

"Sorry, dudes," I said. "You're not going for the softball *or* the tennis ball size. This machine is totally messed up. You have no idea what might happen if you hooked Barry up to it."

"Ask me if I'd care," Andy said sourly.

"I think you would," I said. "Now come on, let's get out of here before someone catches us."

The words had hardly left my lips when we heard the squeak of old bucket wheels out in the hall.

"It's Vlad!" Josh hissed.

18

"*H*ide!" My friends and I ducked behind the blue tarp covering the DITS.

The squeaking grew louder as Vlad pushed the bucket into the science lab. We heard the drip and splash of the wet mop hitting the floor. My friends and I shared a dismal look. It was just our luck that Vlad had decided to mop the science lab while we were hiding in it.

The good news was that it couldn't take very long to mop a classroom, so all we had to do was wait and then sneak out when Vlad was finished.

Beep! Beep! Beep! Beep!

The beeping sound caught us by surprise. For one panicked moment, Josh, Andy, and I all thought it was one of our watches.

But it was Vlad's. We heard another splash as the mop went back into the bucket, then the scrape of chair legs as Vlad sat down. Then a snap as if he'd taken a plastic cap off something.

Still crouched behind the DITS, I stretched up and looked. Vlad was sitting on a chair, drinking from a plastic water bottle.

Only the liquid inside wasn't clear. It was bright red!

I slid back down and felt my heart start to race. My friends gave me worried looks. Andy stretched up, then sank back down with wide, astonished eyes. Josh looked next. In a flash he ducked back down and stared at us with eyes the size of quarters. He moved his lips as if to ask, "What do we do?"

Meanwhile, Andy was breathing faster and faster.

I quickly mouthed the word *chill*. But Andy was really freaking. His eyes darted left and right as if he'd decided to run for it. He started to get up.

Josh and I both grabbed for him. Andy banged into the DITS, making it rattle.

"Vhat is zat?" we suddenly heard Vlad ask. "Is someone here?"

Trembling with fear, my friends and I huddled behind the DITS. We heard the chair legs scrape as Vlad stood up. Then the squeak of the bucket wheels.

I peeked around the DITS. Vlad was coming toward us. He was pushing the mop and bucket ahead of him as if to use them for protection. "Who is zat? Come out!"

Clank! The bucket banged into the DITS. My friends and I popped up and started to run.

"Vhat are you doing here?" Vlad shouted.

Josh and Andy dashed around to the right. I cut to the left, but Vlad pushed the bucket in front of me.

Crash! I fell over the bucket and into Vlad.

Splash! The bucket tipped and the water spilled onto the floor.

Bzzztttt! I heard the sound of electric wires shorting out. The water! The wires on the floor!

Bzzzzzz . . . WHAMP!

Everything went dark.

19

When I opened my eyes, I was lying on the wet science lab floor. The mop water had seeped through my jacket and pants. I could feel it against my skin. I sat up and looked down at myself, expecting to see Vlad's arms and legs. But strangely, I was still in my own body. Meanwhile, Josh and Andy were standing over Vlad, who was lying on his back on the floor.

"Jake, is that you?" Josh asked him.

"No, guys, I'm over here," I said.

Andy and Josh both turned.

"You're still in your body?" Andy asked.

"Looks like it," I said.

"But we heard the *whump*," said Josh.

"Actually, it was more like a *whamp*," said Andy.

"Whatever it was, I guess the DITS didn't work," I said.

Vlad sat up and shook his head. "Vhat happened?"

"Uh, er, nothing," Josh answered.

"I feel strange," Vlad said. "So much, much better."

Meanwhile, I felt weird. Like my arms and legs were extra heavy.

"Come on, Jake, time to leave," Josh said. "We've got a party to go to."

Vlad hardly noticed when we left. We got out of the school and started through the dark. I kept falling behind Josh and Andy.

"What's wrong?" Andy asked.

"I don't know," I answered. "I feel weird. Like, all heavy and slow."

"You probably got a shock when the water hit those wires," Josh said.

"Yeah, you're lucky, Jake," said Andy. "It could have been worse. You could have switched with Vlad."

I knew they were right, but it didn't make me feel any better. We got to my house and went up the walk to the front door.

Grrrrr . . . Woof! Inside the front door, Lance snarled and barked.

"Hey, come on, Lance, it's me," I said.

Grrrrr . . . Woof! Lance barked again and bared his teeth. Through the window we could see the fur on his back standing straight up. His tail was down between his legs.

"What's with him?" Josh asked.

"He's probably just freaked out because of all the trick-or-treaters," Andy said.

"Come on, Jake, open the door," Josh said.

I searched my pocket for a key.

Grrrrr . . . Woof! Lance barked again and looked really angry. Something was definitely weird. Lance never acted this way.

I found my key and handed it to Andy. "Do me a favor? Let yourself in, and then hold Lance's collar tight."

"Why?" Andy asked.

"Just do it," I said.

I waited outside while my friends went in. When Andy had a tight grip on Lance's collar, I came into the house.

Grrrrr . . . Woof! Woof! Woof! Lance lunged at me with his teeth bared. If Andy hadn't pulled him back, I would have been dog food.

"What's going on?" Josh asked.

"I don't know," I said. "Just hold on to Lance while I change into my costume. I'll be right down."

It wasn't easy to climb the stairs. Something was definitely wrong with me. I'd switched bodies enough times before to know that *something* had happened back at school with Vlad. I just wasn't sure what.

I made it to my room. Normally I wouldn't wear a costume, but if I was going to be partners

69

with Amber, I didn't want to look dumb. I happened to have an old black jacket with tails and a tuxedo shirt. If anyone asked, I could say I was dressed up as the famous magician Harry Houdini.

I changed clothes and hurried back downstairs without even bothering to check myself in the mirror.

Grrrrr . . . Woof! Woof! Woof! Lance was still acting like he wanted to kill me. Andy had a hard time holding him back.

"Wait until I get outside," I said. "Then put him in the kitchen and close the door."

"Why?" Andy asked.

"Just do it." I went down the hall and through the kitchen. I could hear loud talking and laughing. Outside there were four times more kids than my friends and I had invited. I hoped it wouldn't be too bad as long as everyone stayed in the backyard.

Amber came through the crowd wearing a small crown on her head and a billowing light blue dress that left her shoulders bare. A thin gold chain hung around her neck and disappeared into the front of the dress. She'd put sparkle makeup around her eyes and was carrying a wand with a star on the end.

"Who are you?" she asked.

"Harry Houdini, the world's most famous magician, at your service, madam." I bowed because I knew Amber liked corny stuff like that.

70

Amber giggled. "Are you ready, Mr. Houdini?"

"Uh, for what?" I asked.

The fine lines across Amber's forehead deepened slightly. "To play Ghost in the Graveyard."

"Oh, right." If I seemed confused it was because I was distracted by a new sensation. It may have been a cool fall evening, but I was starting to feel incredibly thirsty, as if I'd spent the whole day playing soccer in the broiling sun.

"I just need something to drink," I said. "I'll be right back."

Feeling like I was about to die of thirst, I went over to the refreshment table and poured some Coke into a plastic cup. I brought the cup to my lips and . . . *clack*! The edge of the cup banged against something in my mouth. I tried shifting the rim to the other side of my mouth. *Clack!* It banged against something else!

What in the world? I touched my front teeth. Two of them seemed longer than I remembered.

Much longer!

20

I touched the end of one tooth with my finger. It was so pointed it hurt. A cold sweat broke out on my forehead. Something extremely weird was going on. Meanwhile, I was still dying of thirst. I put down the cup and picked up the bottle and gulped as fast as I could.

"Jake?" Someone in a cat disguise tapped me on the shoulder. I jumped around.

"*Ahhh!*" The cat person let out a surprised cry. She had brown hair, long black whiskers on her face, and a tail. I realized it was Julia Sax.

"I'm sorry, Jake," Julia apologized. "You scared me for a moment. Those vampire teeth look so real!"

The better to suck your blood with. Where did that thought come from? Suck blood? What was wrong with me?

"Jake, are you okay?" Julia asked.

"Huh?" I looked up. For a second I'd forgotten she was there.

"I asked if you were okay," Julia said. "You look like . . . I don't know . . . like you just saw a ghost."

"I wish."

"You wish you saw a ghost?" Julia grinned. "Oh, right. Halloween. Wouldn't it be neat?"

Amber in her fairy princess outfit came up. "Ready?" She took my hand and started to lead me into the backyard. Suddenly she stopped and turned.

"Are you okay?" she said.

"Why do you ask?"

She squeezed my hand. "Your hand feels so cold."

"Oh, uh, just bad circulation," I said.

Amber gave me a funny look, then led me to the old plastic playhouse Jessica and I had used when we were little. "I found the best place, Jake. We'll hide here and when anyone comes by we'll jump out and scare them."

We bent down behind the playhouse so people wouldn't see us. Amber was right in front of me. The pale white skin of her neck and shoulders practically glowed in the moonlight. I felt that gnawing thirst again. It didn't make sense. I'd just drunk almost a whole liter of Coke.

The faintest smell of perfume drifted toward me from Amber's bare neck. Her skin looked so perfect, like the skin of a ripe, juicy peach. Was it my imagination, or did the smell of her perfume seem to grow stronger with every passing second? And what was that scent anyway? It promised to be incredibly delicious and thirst-quenching.

I felt myself lean toward her. Thoughts I really didn't want to think jumped into my mind. Thoughts about her pale, soft neck and my pointed, fanglike teeth. *No!* It was wrong! Horribly wrong! And yet I was helpless to stop myself. Amber's neck was drawing me closer and closer. . . .

I was so close that I could almost feel her body heat and her soft, steady breaths. I felt my lips part. It was hopeless. I was under a spell. My body was being controlled by a force far greater than anything I could possibly resist.

My mouth opened wider as I leaned forward. Amber's soft, delicious-looking neck was only inches away. . . .

21

*C*rack! Something hit the backyard fence. Amber twisted around. Her eyes widened with surprise when she saw how close I was. At the same time, the thin gold chain around her neck swung free from her dress, revealing a small gold cross.

"Ugh!" A hoarse grunt of disgust flew from my throat as I lurched backward, covering my eyes. The sight of that gold cross was like deadly radiation.

Crack! Small white fragments of eggshell flew up into the air from the other side of the fence. I went to the backyard gate and pulled it open. Barry Dunn and his buddies were out on the sidewalk with eggs in their hands.

"Look, it's Count Dracula!" Barry laughed.

"I'm Houdini," I said.

"Who Deenie?" Barry repeated with a frown.

"Not Who Deenie. *Houdini.* The most famous magician who ever lived."

"The most famous magician who ever lived was a vampire?" Barry asked.

"No, he was a magician," I said.

"Then how come you're wearing vampire teeth?" Barry asked.

Oops! I'd forgotten. I quickly covered my mouth with my hand. "I'm not. I mean, I am, but not really. Actually I'm Houdini just pretending to be a vampire."

Barry gave me a blank look. "So where's the Super Creamer?"

Uh-oh! I'd forgotten to bring it back from school!

Barry narrowed his eyes menacingly. "You don't have it?"

"I-I'm sorry, Barry," I stammered. "I went to get it and then . . . something happened and . . ."

Barry tossed an egg a few inches in the air and caught it. "You forgot?"

I nodded. Now, in addition to my incredible thirst, I felt a dizzy, sick sensation. I knew what was coming, and it wasn't going to be pretty. I dove for the gate and started to swing it closed behind me.

Splat!

Crack!

Crash!

Even as the gate was closing, half a dozen eggs smashed into it. Raw egg and shell fragments flew everywhere.

"Egg attack!" I shouted.

Eggs began to sail over the fence. The party instantly broke up. Some kids hid behind trees. Others ducked under the refreshment table. Most ran to the side of the house and disappeared.

"What do we do?" Andy yelled from behind a tree as more eggs crashed around us.

"Wait until their supplies run out!" Alex Silver yelled back from behind the house.

Barry and his egg bomber buddies must have heard Alex, because they slowed down the attack. But the eggs still sailed over the fence randomly, and you knew if you moved you might still be hit by one.

Plus, it was possible that if Barry and his buddies detected any movement from within the strike zone they might intensify the attack.

But Barry was craftier than I expected. Now something long, thin, and white shot high into the air and over a tree before plummeting down into my backyard.

"They're switching to toilet paper!" Josh cried, picking up a roll and throwing it back over the fence. Another roll sailed over the fence, leaving another trail of thin white paper through the tree branches.

"Counterattack!" Andy yelled, and threw that roll back.

"No!" I shouted. "Don't throw them back!"

"Why not?" asked Howie Jamison.

"Because you're getting toilet paper all over the place," I said.

"We'll clean it up later," said Josh.

"Yeah," agreed Andy. "This is fun."

A full-scale toilet paper war followed. Every time a roll came in our direction it left another white trail through the branches and across the yard. Kids were running around picking up the rolls and throwing them back. But every time they stepped on unrolled toilet paper, it either stuck to the bottoms of their shoes or got squished into the yard. Even worse, a lot of the toilet paper was starting to stick to the broken eggs on the ground, and when someone stepped on *that* combination it really made a mess!

It wasn't long before the branches of the trees were draped with long white sheets of paper. They looked like huge white balls of cotton candy or pom-poms. The yard was covered with a layer of toilet paper almost as thick as a blanket of snow. Except a lot of what was on the ground was ripped and bunched into dirty white clumps of raw egg and toilet paper and dirt.

The toilet paper war stopped. An eerie stillness filled the dark night air. A few of us stood amid the broken eggs and toilet paper and waited. It felt like we were in a fort out in the Wild West or maybe back in medieval times. We'd withstood the first two rounds of the siege. Would Barry and his fellow attackers give up and go?

Or were they planning yet another fiendish wave?

The answer was an unexpected splash from above. Water sprinkled down on us as if a tiny cloud had suddenly burst. My friends and I stared up at the branches where a moment ago long ribbons of white toilet paper had hung. Now that same toilet paper clung damply to the branches like ugly gray bark.

There was another burst of water in the branches, followed by another.

"Water balloon attack!" Josh cried as a series of green, red, and blue balloons the size of softballs started to rain down, instantly saturating every inch of toilet paper in the trees and on the ground. Everyone ran. I wound up on my hands and knees under the refreshment table with Josh and Andy.

"Remarkable, don't you think?" Josh said.

"What are you talking about?" I asked.

"The order and precision of the attack," he explained. "The eggs as the initial assault, sort of acting as the glue."

"Right," Andy agreed. "And followed by the toilet paper."

Spooosh! A water balloon hit the ground a few feet away, spraying us.

"Exactly," said Josh. "And then the *coup de grâce*! Water balloons."

"For that lasting touch," said Andy.

"It'll take Jake *years* to clean up this mess," Josh chuckled.

"Wait a minute!" I said. "You guys said you'd help."

"We did?" said Andy.

"Yes!" I said. "When I told you not to throw the toilet paper back, and you said you were having too much fun to stop."

"But that was *before* the water balloons," Andy said.

"He's right, Jake," Josh agreed. "If we'd known about the water balloons back then, it would have been a whole different story."

Spooosh! Another balloon exploded on the ground near us. Suddenly we heard someone shout angrily, "What in the world?"

It was Jessica. "Jake?" she called. "Are you out here?"

The water balloon attack had slowed down, so I crawled out from under the refreshment table. "Yes."

"What is going on?" Jessica stood at the kitchen door with her hands on her hips and surveyed the wet toilet paper swamp that had once been our backyard.

"We're being attacked by Barry Dunn," I answered.

"Barry?" Jessica set her jaw angrily. "Jake, open the gate. We'll get Lance to even the score."

"NO!" I screamed. But it was too late. Jessica let Lance out of the kitchen. Lance shot into the backyard like a kamikaze dog. Only he didn't go after Barry Dunn.

He came after me!

22

Nothing makes you forget your other problems faster than being chased up a tree by your own dog.

Grooof! Ruff! Grrrrrrrrr! With his fur up and his teeth bared, Lance stood on his hind legs with his paws against the trunk of the tree I'd just climbed in record time.

Grooof! Ruff! Grrrrrrrrr!

"Chill, Lance, it's just me," I said.

Grooof! Ruff! Grrrrrrrrr! Lance was definitely *not* into chilling.

Jessica, Andy, and Josh joined Lance around the tree and looked up at me with confused expressions on their faces.

"Jake, what is going on?" Jessica asked.

Grooof! Ruff! Grrrrrrrrr!

"Well, uh, Lance chased me up this tree," I said. My hands kept slipping. It's not easy to hold on to branches that are covered with wet toilet paper.

"Yes, Jake, we can see that," Jessica said. "This dog, who has known you since he was a puppy, who has always loved you, who usually can't wait to play with you, has decided for no apparent reason to treat you like you're his worst enemy ever."

"I'd say that about sums it up," I said.

My sister shook her head wearily. "Okay, Jake, what do we do now?"

"Put Lance back in the house," I said. "No, wait. Even better. Keep Lance out here, and I'll go in the house."

"What about this incredible mess?" Jessica waved her arm around the backyard.

"We'll get to that later," I said. "But first, one of you should take Lance for a walk so I can get out of this tree."

Andy volunteered. Even after he clipped the leash to Lance's collar, it took a lot of pulling to get our dog away from the tree.

As soon as Andy and Lance left, I climbed down.

"I thought you hated dressing up in costumes," my sister said as we started back toward the house.

"I'm Houdini," I said.

Jessica scowled. "Then what's with the fangs?"

"I'm Houdini pretending to be a vampire."

My sister let out a long, weary sigh. "It's hard

to believe that we actually come from the same parents."

"Gee, Jessica," Josh chuckled, "I thought you were going to say it was hard to believe you two come from the same *planet*."

"That, too," my sister agreed.

We crossed the yard. I pulled the kitchen door open and went in. Jessica followed and Josh closed the door behind us. The kitchen was brightly lit. I glanced at one of the windows and saw Josh's and Jessica's reflection.

Something wasn't right.

I looked at another window and saw the reflection of my sister and my friend.

I quickly looked at yet another window.

And then another.

In every window I could clearly see the reflection of Josh and Jessica.

But in none of those windows could I see me.

23

"I have to use the bathroom." I hurried out of the kitchen and into the powder room. Inside I switched on the light and locked the door.

The powder room mirror was smudged with my sister's toothpaste-foam spots and streaks. But as I stared past them and into the mirror itself, all I saw was an empty bathroom. It was like looking through a window into another room.

I felt cold sweat break out on my forehead again. If I was looking into a mirror and all I was seeing was an empty bathroom, then where was I?

Something very weird had happened with the DITS. In the past, I had switched bodies. But this time I was still in my own body. Only something was in my body with me, and that something was making me look and act like a vampire.

Was it possible that a vampire was trapped inside of me? Or that my body had become a vampire's body and now I was trapped in it?

And what did Vlad the custodian have to do with all this?

Rap! Rap! Someone knocked on the bathroom door. "Jake?" It was Josh. "You better come out. Barry's back."

I left the powder room and followed Josh down the hall. Barry and his buddies were in our front yard "rolling" the trees and bushes with toilet paper. Jessica was standing on the walk yelling at them.

"You stop right now or I'm going to call your mother," she shouted.

Barry blasted her with a can of shaving cream. I have to hand it to Jessica. A lot of kids would get "creamed" in the face and turn and run, but not my sister. Catching Barry by surprise, she grabbed the can out of his hand and creamed him right back!

Barry laughed and started to run, as if it were a game. He didn't know that Jessica has a great arm. She can throw a football just about as far, hard, and accurately as any kid I know. Gripping the can of shaving cream like a football, Jessica threw a perfect spiral bullet.

Bonk! The can hit Barry in the back of the head. Still running, he started to fall forward, flailing his arms as he tried to keep his balance.

Clonk! He smashed headfirst into a telephone pole and went down. Then he rolled over and sat on the ground holding his head.

24

A couple of Barry's buddies ran over to see if he was okay. They helped him to his feet. Barry looked wobbly at first, but then his lips pursed together angrily and he balled his hands into fists. He looked about as angry as I'd ever seen him.

And he was staring right at Jessica.

Josh glanced at me. "If you're hoping Barry won't hurt Jessica because she's a girl, forget it. Barry's a politically correct bully. If he's mad enough, he'll beat up anyone. And right now he's definitely mad enough."

I knew I had to do something. Jessica had only been trying to protect our house. None of this would have happened if I hadn't decided to break the rules and have a party. I knew I had to scare Barry off, but I couldn't do it with my bare hands. I needed a stick or a bat.

Barry started toward my sister.

"You better do something fast or she's going to get it bad." Josh turned and looked for me. "Jake? Where are you?"

Josh would have seen me if he'd known where to look. Straight up above him in the dark night sky. I didn't know how I got up there, but I was looking down at the top of Josh's head as he turned it this way and that to find me.

"Jake? Jeez, Jake, where'd you go?"

I didn't have time to answer. Barry was storming toward Jessica with fire in his eyes. I went toward them. I guess that meant I was flying.

Only how could I be flying in Jake Sherman's body?

I guess you've figured that part out.

I wasn't in *my* body.

I was in this *other* body. A brown, furry body with pointy ears and long, skinny wings.

Sounds pretty batty, right? And it wasn't like I knew how to fly or anything! *Watch out below! Bombs away!*

"*AHHHHHHHH!*" It was Jessica who saw me first. Or maybe I should say, *heard* me first. Since I was making an awful lot of noise flapping my wings to stay up in the air.

If there's one thing that Jessica really, *really* hates, it's furry flying animals with claws, whiskers, and wings. Especially when they're flying straight toward her.

"Go away!" She waved frantically as if I were a big horsefly or something.

Wait a minute. Jessica wasn't the one I wanted. I wanted Barry. Still flopping and flapping, I tried to twist around in midair.

Barry had forgotten about my sister and was gaping up at me. "Get away! Shoo!" He started to wave his arms frantically, too. By now I was getting into flying mode. It was actually fun! I mean, who hasn't dreamed of flying? The limitless freedom . . . the feeling of the wind in your face. I curved around and dive-bombed Barry again!

"Help!" Barry screamed, and started to run. "It's after me! Help!"

This was great! All I had to do was fly around Barry's head and I'd scare him silly!

Barry ran as fast as he could. Suddenly he skidded to a stop and picked something up off the ground. He spun around and aimed a can of shaving cream at me. The next thing I knew, the air in front of me was filled with white foam. I banked hard to the left.

Too late! I flew straight into a glob of shaving cream.

Splat! It got me right in the face! Now I couldn't see a thing! My bat sonar was all gummed up!

Mayday! Mayday! Air alert! Incoming! Out of control!

Lesson number one of bat flying: You can't wipe shaving cream off your face when you're in the air!

Whoa! Look out! Foam the runway! Red alert! Man overboard!

CRASH!

25

*G*rrruuufff! Woooffff! Grrrrrrrr!
  I was lying on my back. The ground under
me felt soft, damp, and cold.

My head throbbed painfully. A dog was barking
in my ear.

I opened my eyes and looked up through tree
branches at the stars in the dark night sky above.

Grrruuufff! Woooffff! Grrrrrrrr! I turned my
head and saw Lance's bared teeth as he barked at
me.

I winced. Wow, did my head hurt. I reached up
and felt it. Ow! I had a bump the size of a golf ball.

Hey, wait a minute! Since when did I have a
head? And a hand? Where did the bat go?

Grrruuufff! Woooffff! Grrrrrrrr! Lance kept
barking, but I had a feeling that as long as I didn't
try to get up he wouldn't attack. I heard voices.

"Lance, what are you barking at? Is someone
out here?"

Now I could see the silhouette of someone coming toward me in the dark. It was Andy.

"Hey, over here!" he called, and then kneeled down beside me. "Jake, you okay?"

Josh and Jessica arrived and kneeled beside me, their faces etched with concern.

"Jake, what happened?" Andy asked. "What are you doing back here? How'd you get that shaving cream on your face?"

"I-I don't know," I lied.

Grrrrrrrrrrrrrr! Lance growled again.

"Josh, could you take Lance into the house and put him in my room?" my sister asked.

"Sure, but after that I have to go," Josh said. "It's getting kind of late. See you tomorrow, Jake, okay?"

He took Lance by the collar and led him into the house. Andy and Jessica helped me to my feet.

"You won't believe what you missed," Andy said excitedly. "Jessica hit Barry in the back of the head with a can of shaving cream. He came after her with total murder in his eyes, and just when you thought it was good-bye, Jessica, this huge bat shows up. Like the one we saw last night when we went looking for the cow!"

I was only half listening. Mostly I was surveying the mess. The inside of the house wasn't too bad. Just a lot of empty soda bottles and candy bags. But the outside was a disaster. The backyard was a toilet-paper-and-raw-egg swamp. The trees were covered with toilet paper, and shaving cream and empty cans were all over the place.

"Jake, I don't know why I should lift a finger to help you," Jessica said as we stopped in the kitchen. "But some weird older sister complex doesn't want me to let you get the punishment you so richly deserve."

"I appreciate it," I said.

"Good, now grab a rake and come out front and help clean." Jessica opened the kitchen closet and pulled out a bunch of dark green garbage bags and headed down the hall.

"I guess we better help her," Andy said.

"Wait, Andy," I said. "I have a problem."

"I'll say," Andy agreed. "If you don't get this place cleaned up, your parents are gonna come home and kill you."

"It's worse than that," I said.

Andy frowned. "Worse than your parents killing you?"

I pointed at my two long teeth. "See these?"

"Yeah?"

"They don't come out."

"What are you talking about?" Andy asked.

"They're real."

"Yeah, right," Andy scoffed. "Like you just grew them tonight."

"Exactly."

Andy shook his head in annoyed disbelief. "What is with you, Jake?"

I pointed at the kitchen window. "What do you see, Andy?"

"A window," he answered.

"What's *in* the window?"

"A reflection of me and —" My friend's voice trailed off.

"You and what?" I asked.

"Where are you?" Andy gasped.

"Right here," I answered.

Andy looked at me and then back at the window. "Yeah, but —"

"You starting to get the picture?" I asked.

Andy's eyes went wide. He began to pull junk out of his pockets. Crumpled-up candy wrappers, loose change, a key, and then a small white clove of garlic, which he held out toward me. "Stay away!"

26

"I'm not going to do anything to you," I said.

"Don't move." Andy backed away. His hand was trembling.

"Wait," I said.

"Don't come near me!"

"Chill, Andy. I'm your friend."

"Friend?" Andy laughed. "Ha! Vampires have no friends, Jake."

"I'm not a vampire!" I insisted.

"Oh, really? You've got fangs and no reflection."

"You don't really believe in that stuff, do you?" I asked.

"Oh, yeah. Big-time." Andy was still backing away.

"Seriously, Andy, you can't leave," I said. "I need you."

"I bet!" Andy cried. "But I have news for you, Mr. I'm-Not-a-Vampire. I like my blood just as much as you do. Except it's mine and I intend to keep it. All of it!"

"Please, Andy," I begged. "I don't know what's wrong with me, but if you leave me here, I'm dead."

"If you're one of *them*, you already are dead!" He turned and started to sprint down the hall toward the front door. I couldn't let him get away. He was the only person I knew who knew anything about vampires.

"Come back!" I yelled, and started after him. There was no way I could catch him by running. He was too far ahead. I only had one chance.

Bat! Bat! Bat! I thought as hard as I could.

The next thing I knew I was flying down the hall. Andy was still about ten feet from the front door when it suddenly opened and Jessica stormed in, looking upset.

"You have some nerve, Jake!" she started to yell. "I said I'd help you clean up, but if you think I'm going to do it all by myself, you're —"

She stopped and stared at Andy coming down the hall toward her and then at me in MegaBat's body flying above him.

"*Ahhhhhhhh!*" my sister screamed, and slammed the door. A split second later I landed in front of the door and instantly turned back into Jake.

Andy skidded to a stop.

"I swear I'm not going to hurt you," I said.

Andy quickly held up the clove of garlic. "Stay away!"

"I need your help, Andy."

"You need my blood," he replied in a trembling voice.

"Not if you help me," I said.

"How?"

"Remember you said that some people thought this vampire stuff might be caused by a disease or a vitamin deficiency?" I said.

"Yeah?"

"Well, which is it?" I asked.

"Which is what?" he asked back.

"A disease or a vitamin deficiency?" I said.

Andy's eyes darted left and right as if he was desperately searching for an escape route.

"Come on, Andy, help me," I pleaded.

"Well, uh, if it's a disease, I don't know what to tell you," he said. "I mean, you can try going to the doctor, but I'm not sure what he's gonna say if you tell him you need to be cured of being a vampire."

"What if it's a vitamin deficiency?" I asked.

"Well, er, I guess you'd have to take some vitamins," he answered.

"We don't have any," I said. That was one thing about my family, we weren't into vitamins and health food.

"How about V8 juice?" Andy asked. "That's supposed to have a lot of vitamins in it."

V8 juice? I was pretty sure there was an old bottle somewhere in the refrigerator. I headed back toward the kitchen. As I passed Andy, he held up that stupid clove of garlic.

"Would you give that a rest already?" I said.

Andy lowered the garlic. "It doesn't work?"

"I *told* you," I snapped irritably. "I'm *not* a vampire!"

"Right," Andy mumbled as he followed me into the kitchen. "You've got fangs, no reflection, and you can turn yourself into a bat. It's just part of being a teenager? Some kids get zits, Jake gets fangs."

"You got it." I pulled opened the refrigerator. The bottle was way in the back, next to the open box of baking powder.

"Wow, that's one old bottle of V8 juice," Andy remarked.

"How can you tell?" I asked.

"Are you kidding? It's got dust on it. You know how long something has to be in the refrigerator to collect dust? You sure you want to drink it?"

It was a good question. But Andy didn't know how desperate I was. I was dying of thirst. I was ready to do . . . *anything*! Andy probably hadn't washed his grubby neck in a month, but I had no doubt that I'd bite it if that dusty old bottle of V8 didn't work.

I twisted off the cap, lifted the bottle to my lips, and chugged.

Gross! I didn't like the taste of V8 when it was fresh! This stuff tasted prehistoric! Forget about the dust on the *outside* of the bottle. It tasted like it was half dust on the *inside*!

With a pause or two to catch my breath, I managed to finish the whole bottle.

"Wow, you really must have been thirsty," Andy said.

I nodded and waited to feel something change inside of me. But nothing happened. I still felt parched.

It was hopeless.

I was lost to the dark side.

"Jake?" Andy said nervously.

I fixed my eyes on him. More specifically, on his neck. It had a ring of dirt around it, as if it hadn't been washed in years. But that no longer mattered. To me, the only thing that mattered was what pulsed just beneath his grimy skin.

27

Andy swallowed nervously. "Jake, what is it? What's wrong?"

Wrong? Nothing was wrong. In fact, everything was right. Right for a bite. I fixed my gaze on his eyes.

"What are you doing, Jake?" Andy asked in a quavering voice. "Why are you looking at me like that?"

I didn't answer. I just stared. I was no longer in control of myself. Some other force had taken over. A force so strong all I could do was obey.

"J-Jake?" Andy looked dazed. His legs quivered as if he wanted to run but couldn't. Like a snake hypnotizing its prey, I knew I had him. Andy and his dirty neck were mine. All mine!

Rummmble . . . We heard thunder. Raindrops started to splat against the windows. *Bang!* The front door slammed.

A moment later Jessica tiptoed nervously into the kitchen. "Is it gone?"

"What?" I asked.

"The bat," my sister said. "And what was it doing in the house anyway?"

Andy and I stared at each other. I blinked both eyes hard as if I'd just awakened from a spell. That incredible thirst had gone!

Jessica picked up the empty bottle of V8 juice. "You drank this?"

I nodded.

"You okay?" Andy asked.

"I-I think so," I answered uncertainly.

"You may think so now," Jessica said. "But just wait until Mom and Dad get home and see that mess outside."

Rummmble . . . There was more thunder.

"There's a big storm coming," Jessica said. "It's supposed to pour all night."

"I better get home," Andy said. He hurried down the hall and out of the house.

A minute later it started to pour.

"Too late now to clean up," Jessica said. "Good night, Jake. I'm going to bed."

28

The wind howled and the rain flew sideways through the dark night sky. It was way after midnight. I sat on my bed, touching my fangs with my finger and wondering what would happen to me. I went over and stood in front of the mirror. Once again, an empty room stared back at me. Then I had a thought I never, ever imagined possible: Thank God for V8!

I spent most of the night playing computer games. Sometime around five in the morning, I glanced up at the window and noticed just the slightest hint of brightening in the dark sky. Dawn was coming.

Once again I felt myself driven by forces I didn't understand. I shut the blinds as tight as possible, crawled into bed, and pulled the blankets over my head.

29

It felt like the middle of the night when the sound of voices woke me under my cocoon of blankets.

"Jake, you in there?" It sounded like Andy.

"What's that lump in the bed?" That sounded like Josh.

"I bet that's him," Andy said.

I felt a finger poke the blankets. "That you, Jake?"

"Hmmmm," I answered with an annoyed grunt. I felt groggy and grumpy about being awakened from a deep sleep.

"Why's it so dark in here?" Josh asked.

I heard the sound of a shade opening. Even in my deep burrow of blankets, I sensed just the faintest glimmer of light.

"Close that shade!" I shouted with an anger that surprised me as much as my friends.

"Okay, okay," Josh said. "Gee, Jake, what's with you?"

"Sounds like he's in a bad mood," Andy added.

"You should be happy, Jake," Josh said. "At least you don't have that huge mess to clean up."

Huh? "What happened?" I asked from my blanket cocoon.

"Didn't you hear the storm last night?" Josh asked. "The wind and rain washed everything away. You'd never even know there'd been a party. Come on, you have to get up and see." I felt him tug at my blankets.

"Don't touch my blankets!" I screamed. Once again, I couldn't understand where the anger in my voice was coming from. "And keep the windows closed and the lights off."

Josh let go. "Jeez, what's with him?" he asked.

"Well, uh, there's something I didn't tell you," Andy said. Hushed whispering followed.

"What?" Josh cried.

There were more hushed whispers.

"Are you crazy?" Josh asked.

And more whispering.

"But how?" Josh wondered.

More whispering.

"No kidding?"

More whispering.

"Well, okay," Josh said after a while. "Maybe he is a vampire. But he doesn't have to be so grumpy about it."

"Ahem," Andy cleared his throat. "You know, Jake, you can't stay under those blankets all day.

I mean, not if you want to do anything about this little, er, problem of yours."

"Leave me alone," I growled.

"Sure," Andy said. "But it's not going to work. Your parents are going to come back, and I really don't think they're gonna understand when you want to stay up all night and sleep all day."

"Bah." *Huh?* I'd never said *bah* before in my life!

"Let's look at this in another way," Andy said. "There's no school today, but the school's open. We all know this has something to do with the DITS and Vlad. If that's true, this could be your only chance to change back."

"You could be right," I replied. "But how can I go to school? I can't even come out from under these blankets."

"Maybe you can," said Andy.

"What are you talking about, Andy?" Josh asked. "You know vampires can't go out in the sun."

"I know that *used* to be true," Andy replied. "But that was before SPF 45."

30

I don't know if you've ever tried to put on All-Day SPF 45 Waterproof Sunblock while you're still in bed, but it isn't easy.

"How's it going?" Andy asked from outside my cocoon of blankets.

"I'm getting more sunblock on the sheets than I am on me," I answered. My little cocoon was starting to feel like the inside of a glove filled with Vaseline.

"Just make sure you get it all over," Andy advised me.

"How do you know if this is even gonna work?" I asked.

"We'll do a test," Andy suggested. "You stick the part of your body you least need out from under the blanket. If it doesn't fall off or disintegrate, we'll know."

"What part of my body do I least need?" I asked.

"Your head," said Josh.

"Very funny," I muttered.

"No, like a foot or something," Andy said.

"I hate to tell you this, but I happen to need my feet," I said. "I'm not sacrificing one just to see if this stupid idea works."

"What about an elbow?" Josh suggested.

"Oh, great," I groaned. "Suppose I stick my elbow out and it falls off? Then what happens to my hand?"

"I'll give you a hand," Josh joked.

"You're *so* not funny."

"Try a pinkie," Andy suggested. "Go a digit at a time. That way, the most you can lose is a couple of fingers."

"Thanks, Andy, I feel a whole lot better now," I grumbled sarcastically and slowly slid my hand toward the edge of the blankets until I felt my pinkie slide out into the air.

"Oh, gross!" Andy cried.

"It's horrible!" yelled Josh.

31

I jerked my hand back under the blanket and felt it. My pinkie was still there.

Andy and Josh started to laugh.

"What's so funny?" I asked from under the covers.

"We fooled you!" Josh chuckled. "There was nothing wrong with your pinkie!"

"Yeah, come on, Jake," Andy agreed. "We were just kidding around. Stick it out again."

"I could kill you guys."

"We know you could," said Andy. "That's another reason we want you to change back to your old self. No offense or anything, but we don't need any vampires as friends."

I stuck my pinkie out.

"All systems go for another finger," Andy said.

I stuck out my ring finger.

"Think he should go for the whole hand?" Josh asked.

"Definitely," Andy agreed.

I pushed my hand out from under the blanket.

"Looking good!" Josh yelled. "Do we try for the elbow?"

"Go, elbow!" Andy urged me.

I stretched my arm until it was out all the way up to the elbow.

"We have elbow!" Josh announced.

"Jake, I think it's safe to assume this is gonna work," Andy said. "The only things I'm still worried about are your eyes."

"He needs shades," Josh said. I heard a drawer squeak open. "You want the Ray · Bans or the Oakleys?"

"The Ray · Bans'll be fine," I said.

Josh placed them in my hand, and I pulled them into my greasy cocoon.

"Okay, Jake, you ready?" Andy asked.

"I guess," I answered.

"You sure you got sunblock everywhere?" Josh asked. "Even between your toes?"

"Bottoms of your feet?" asked Andy.

"Behind your ears?" added Josh.

"In your armpits?" said Andy.

"Up your nose?" said Josh.

"I don't need sunblock up my nose," I said.

"You sure?" Andy asked. "I'd hate to see your nose fall off."

"I guess it depends how much light can get up in there," Josh said. "Knowing Jake's nose, it's probably so full of boogers he doesn't have to worry."

"Save it, guys, I'm not in the mood." I climbed out from the blankets and stood in the dim light of my room.

"I think this is gonna work." Andy went into my closet and tossed me a pair of pants and a long-sleeved shirt.

"You okay, Jake?" Josh asked, studying me closely. "You look kind of pale."

"I *feel* kind of pale," I replied.

"That reminds me." Andy opened his backpack and pulled out a twelve-ounce can of V8. "I brought some just in case." He tossed me the can. I hooked my finger through the tab.

"Wait." Josh gave me a sheepish look. "I was just wondering. With those fangs, couldn't you bite right into the can? I mean, why bother popping the top?"

I glanced at Andy.

"It *would* be pretty cool," he said.

"You guys are so demented."

"Come on, please?" Josh begged.

"Oh, okay." I took a moment to find the best place on the can to bite. Finally I held it upright and bit near the bottom. My fangs easily pierced the thin aluminum, and I tasted the V8 as I started to drink.

"Mad cool!" Josh grinned.

Andy just stared in amazement.

"Had your thrill?" I asked as I tossed the empty can in the garbage. My friends both nodded. Josh even reached into the garbage and picked up the can. A few drops of V8 dripped out of the two fang holes.

"What are you doing?" I asked.

"Souvenir," Josh answered. He shook the last drops off and pocketed the can. We left my room and headed downstairs. Andy stopped by the front closet.

"Just to be safe, I think we ought to give you some more protection." He took out a coat, gloves, a black scarf, and a hat with a wide brim.

I put everything on and wrapped the scarf around my face. Why take chances?

"Perfect." Andy scanned me from head to toe. "I can't see a single inch of skin. With those wrap-around glasses, the hat, and the scarf, you're totally covered."

"Now what?" a voice asked behind us.

We turned to see Jessica coming down the hall from the kitchen. She stopped and squinted at me. "Halloween was yesterday, Jake."

"We really have to fly," Andy said, taking my arm.

Jessica wrinkled her nose and sniffed. "Sunblock?"

"You never know," Andy said, pulling me out the door.

32

Outside I looked around in amazement. Andy was right. It had rained so hard the night before that almost every trace of shaving cream and toilet paper had been washed away. A few wet toilet paper shreds still hung in the tree branches, but unless you were looking for them, you probably wouldn't notice.

That was a relief. Unfortunately, I still had big problems. I was starting to feel thirsty again. Without intending to, I found myself gazing hungrily at Andy's neck.

"Hey, what's with you?" Andy asked.

"Oh, nothing." I quickly looked away.

"You were staring at my neck," Andy said.

"No, I wasn't."

"Yes, you were."

"How would you know?" I asked defensively. "You can't see my eyes under these glasses."

"Here." Andy dug into his backpack, came up

with another can of V8, and tossed it to me. "Drink."

"This is gross," I protested. "V8 for breakfast?"

"You'd prefer blood?" Josh asked.

"Shut up." I slid my finger through the tab.

"Wait," Andy said. "Don't I get a souvenir, too?"

I bit into the can and drained it in no time. I tossed it to Andy, and we started toward school.

The storm had passed, but it was still overcast and gray. Brown and orange leaves lay wet and heavy on the streets and lawns, and squirrels were collecting acorns.

The parking lot at school was filled with teachers' cars.

"Now what?" Josh asked. "It's not like we can just stroll in. Someone's gonna wonder what we're doing."

"Let's go around to the science wing," Andy said. "Maybe we can get in without anyone seeing us."

We started around toward the back, and soon came across one of the most amazing sights we'd ever seen.

33

It may have been a cold, gray, and windy day, but out behind the school someone was relaxing on a lounge chair. And he was wearing only an orange bathing suit. He lay back with his hands behind his head and a big smile on his face. Next to the lounge chair was a small table with a bottle of soda and a boom box on it.

My friends and I walked up to him. Vlad didn't see or hear us. His eyes were closed, and he was listening to a Zombies song on the classic rock station.

"Enjoying yourself?" Andy asked.

Vlad's eyes popped open with surprise. "What are you doing here?"

"Looking for the bloodsucking bum who turned our friend Jake into a, er, bloodsucking bum," Josh said, trying to sound tough.

Vlad's eyes widened. "So zat is vhat happened?"

"Right, and zat is vhat is going to unhappen, too," Josh said.

"Vhat do you mean?" Vlad asked.

"He means ve vant you and Jake to switch back to the vay things vere," Andy explained.

Vlad's jaw dropped, and he shook his head in terror. "No! Never!" He jumped out of the lounge chair. "I can't! You don't know vhat it vas like! It vas horrible!"

"So you think it's fair that you gave it to me?" I asked.

"Fair?" Vlad cried. "You think it vas fair zat some creep gave it to me? You think it's fair zat for the last twenty years I should never see the sun, or zat I should have to drink zat terrible V8 juice every single day?"

"You, too?" I asked, amazed.

"Of course!" Vlad said. "You tink I vant to go around biting people on the neck and drinking their blood? It's so unsanitary!"

Vlad turned off the boom box and started to fold up the lounge chair.

"Wait, where are you going?" Andy cried.

"To the tanning place in town," Vlad answered, pointing at the pale white skin on his arm. "Look at dis. I'm out here all morning and not a bit of tan. Not one bit! And it's freezing, too."

"Most people get tan in the summer," Josh said, "not the day after Halloween."

"Dey haven't been vaiting twenty years!" Vlad shoved the lounge chair under one arm, picked up his boom box, and stomped off toward the school.

115

"Now what do we do?" I moped.

"Think we could somehow trick Vlad into switching?" Josh asked.

Andy shook his head. "Forget it. He won't go near the DITS again for as long as he lives."

"Then I'll never get to switch back," I moaned in despair.

"It's not like you really switched in the first place," Josh pointed out. "You're still Jake."

"But I'm a vampire!" I wailed.

"Wait, let's think about this," Andy said. "Usually when someone becomes a vampire it's because they've been bitten by a vampire."

"Right," I said, "but when that happens the biter is still a vampire, too."

"So what the DITS did was take the vampire out of Vlad and put it in you," said Josh.

"Exactly."

"That's it!" Andy said brightly. "Then all we have to do is find someone to give the vampire in you to."

"Barry Dunn!" Josh cried.

"Perfect!" said Andy.

"No way." I shook my head. "If you think he picks on us a lot now, just wait until he also needs our blood."

Josh rubbed his chin. "Good point."

"What about Amanda Gluck?" Andy asked.

"That means one of these nights someone is going to wake up and find her sucking on their neck," I predicted.

Josh made a face. "Gross!"

"Yeah, forget that," Andy agreed. "Amanda would probably love being a vampire. We'd be doing her a favor."

My friends and I thought about it some more.

"I hate to say this, Jake," Andy said at last. "But I can't think of anyone you should switch with."

"Then I'll be a vampire for the rest of my life!" I cried. "Drinking V8 juice. Never seeing the sun. Never going to the beach."

"You'll get to watch a lot of late-night television," Josh pointed out.

"No fights with Jessica over who gets the remote," added Andy.

"Thanks a lot, guys," I sniffed.

"You want to know the truth?" Andy asked. "It's just not fair to turn someone else into a vampire. I mean, think about how you feel, Jake. Anyone you give this to is gonna feel that way, also."

"So I have to spend the rest of my life as a vampire," I whined.

"Unless we can think of something else to give it to," Josh said.

"You mean, like a dog?" Andy asked. "We know we can switch with Lance because Jake and I have both done it."

"No way," I said. "I'm not turning Lance into a vampire dog."

"It's better than giving it to a person," Josh said.

"Forget it," I said. "Lance'll never drink V8, and that means he'll only want the real stuff."

"You're right." Andy's shoulders sagged. "And he's fast and strong so he'll be able to get it."

Josh hung his head. "Forget it, Jake. We might as well go home."

I knew he was right. It was hopeless. It was my bad luck, and I'd just have to learn to live with it. Or at least be undead with it. Josh and I started to walk.

"Look on the bright side, Jake," he said. "There's got to be a way you can use this."

"Use what?" I asked.

"The fang thing," Josh said. "Like on a commercial or something. Maybe Tang. You could say, 'I've got a fang for Tang.' "

"You're not serious."

"How about — "

"Guys!" Andy shouted behind us.

Josh and I looked back.

Andy was jumping up and down. "I've got it! Come on!" He turned and started to run back behind the school.

34

"This better be good," Josh said. As we came around the side of the building, we heard clanging.

"Come on, you sweet little cutie." Andy was talking the World's Ugliest Cross-eyed Cow out of the shed.

"What are you doing?" Josh asked.

"This is the answer," Andy said. "We need to switch the vampire out of Jake and into something that can't hurt people. Something that's really slow and makes a lot of noise so people will know it's coming."

"You're going to turn her into the World's Ugliest Cross-eyed Vampire Cow?" I gasped.

"Andy's right," said Josh. "Given the choice between Jake the Vampire, Lance the Vampire, Barry the Vampire, and the World's Ugliest Vampire Cow —"

Clang! The World's Ugliest Cross-eyed Cow

followed Andy toward the doors at the back of the science wing.

"What about the teachers?" I asked.

"They're over in the cafetorium," Andy said. "Just pray they don't hear us."

We led the World's Ugliest Cross-eyed Cow into the science wing and then into Mr. Dirksen's room.

"First we have to re-create the conditions from when you switched with Vlad," Andy said, ducking behind the DITS. "Josh, go fill a big beaker with water. Jake, you hold on to the cow."

I watched as Andy spread some of the wires on the floor.

"Got the water." Josh came back with a beaker.

"Okay, let's do it," Andy said. "Jake, come closer with the cow. Josh, spill the water over the wires."

Bzzzzztttt!

WHUMP!

35

Something was wrong. It wasn't the *whamp!* I'd heard when I'd gotten the vampire germs from Vlad. It was the *WHUMP!* I usually heard when people switched bodies. And when I opened my eyes I wasn't lying on the floor, either.

I couldn't see anything because the lab had filled with a cloud of water vapor, but I had a funny taste in my mouth. Sort of like hay. And I could feel something heavy around my neck.

The fog started to clear. Across the room, Andy and Josh were standing with someone who looked exactly like me.

"Jake?" Andy was saying. "Jake, can you hear me?"

Jake didn't answer. He just stood there with a blank expression on his face.

"What's wrong with him?" Josh asked.

"I don't know," Andy said. "Come on, Jake, say something. Just let us know you're okay."

Jake opened his mouth. *"Moooooooooooo!"*

Josh turned to Andy. "You idiot! You switched Jake with the World's Ugliest Cross-eyed Cow!"

My friends rushed over to me in the body of the World's Ugliest Cross-eyed Cow.

"Jake, you in there?" Josh asked.

I nodded the cow's head. The cowbell clanged.

"I don't believe this." Andy swallowed.

Both he and Josh looked really upset. Personally, I didn't see what the big problem was. It wasn't so bad being a cow. You didn't have to go anywhere. And with all these stomachs full of cud you would always have something to eat. What more did anyone need?

"We have to try it again," Andy said. "You get Jake. I'll set up the DITS again."

Andy didn't have to worry about getting me in the cow's body, because I hadn't gone anywhere. Why bother moving? I had my cud. Things were cool. Being in a cow's body was a very mellow experience.

Across the room, Josh took Jake's hand and tried to lead him back toward the DITS. Only, Jake wouldn't budge.

"Not this again!" Josh fumed.

"You have to talk nice," Andy said.

Josh rolled his eyes. "Darling Jake, or Mrs. Cow, or whoever you are. Would you please delight me with your company back at the DITS so that I might have the pleasure of switching you back into your own ugly cross-eyed cow body?"

122

A smile actually appeared on my face. The World's Ugliest Cross-eyed Cow was happy that Josh had spoken nicely. In my body she slowly followed Josh back to the DITS. Josh looked back over his shoulder.

"You could walk a little faster," he muttered.

"She doesn't know that," Andy said.

"This isn't the World's Ugliest Cross-eyed Cow, it's the World's Stupidest, Ugliest Cross-eyed Cow," Josh grumbled.

Whack! The cow in my body smacked Josh in the back of the head and sent him staggering across the room.

"Ow!" Josh yelped. "Why'd you do that?"

"Maybe she isn't so stupid after all." Andy grinned.

A moment later, they were ready to try again. Josh splashed the water on the floor.

Bzzzzzzt!

WHUMP!

36

Oh, no! It was the wrong sound again!

"It's okay, everyone!" Andy called out in the fog, as if he could read our minds. "We had to switch Jake and the cow back before we can go on to the next step!"

Phew! Even though the room was still filled with fog, I quickly slid my hands over my head and arms and legs. I was back in my own body!

"Hold on!" Andy yelled. "More water!"

Splash!

Bzzzzzzt!

WHAMP! That was the sound I remembered.

Moowwwwooooooooooooooo! The loud anguished cry from the World's Ugliest Cross-eyed Cow caught me by surprise.

Clop! Clop!

Clang! Clang!

"She's on the move!" Andy cried.

The World's Ugliest Cross-eyed Cow barreled past me and out of the lab. My friends and I followed her out into the hall. She got to the exit door, shoved it open with her nose, and then clomped out. She trundled across the athletic fields and toward the woods, the clanging of her bell growing fainter and fainter until she vanished among the trees.

Josh, Andy, and I stood at the doors and watched. When she was gone, Josh turned to me. "Still feel like a vampire?"

I reached up and touched my teeth. My fangs were gone. "I don't think so."

"You sure?" Andy asked.

"Let me see your neck," I said.

Andy pulled the collar of his shirt away from his neck, revealing the spot I'd once longed for. I gazed at the dirty, grimy skin . . . and felt totally grossed out.

"Yeah," I said. "I'm okay."

37

Josh and Andy wanted to go to the mall, but I had to go home and take a shower to get all the sunblock off. I also had to wash my bedclothes so my parents wouldn't wonder why my bed was full of sunblock.

Mom and Dad got home around dinnertime. They looked really glad that the house was still standing and hadn't been destroyed.

I hadn't slept much in the past thirty-six hours. After dinner, I went upstairs and got into bed. I fell asleep almost instantly.

It must have been the middle of the night when I was awakened by a growl. I opened my eyes. My room was dark and the house was quiet.

Grrrrrrrrrr! It was Lance downstairs. Usually when he growled like that it meant he'd sensed something outside. Probably just someone out for a late-night walk.

Grrrrrrrrr! Grooof! He barked. That was really unusual for late at night.

As tired as I was, I dragged myself out of bed.

Groof! Groof! Something was definitely bothering Lance, and if I didn't go see what it was he'd probably wake up the whole house.

I trudged downstairs. Lance was in the kitchen with his nose pressed to the door. I opened it and let him out.

Groof! Groof! Groof! Lance bounded into the dark. I peered through the window, trying to see.

Clang! Clang! From out of the dark came the ghostly white face of the World's Ugliest Cross-eyed Cow!

Only there was something different about her. It took me a second to realize what it was. The World's Ugliest Cross-eyed Cow now had two long white fangs!

Groof! Groof! Groof! Lance barked and nipped at her hooves.

The World's Ugliest Cross-eyed Vampire Cow shook her head and started to shrink and change form . . . into a bat!

Groof? Lance looked up, puzzled, as the World's Ugliest Cross-eyed Vampire Cow-Bat spread its wings and rose into the sky.

I felt a hot shiver of fear as it took flight, a black outline flapping against the moon. The

World's Ugliest Cross-eyed Vampire Cow was going someplace new.

Who knows where?

Maybe somewhere close to where you live.

If it's dark out and you hear a *Clang!* . . .

Beware.

And keep some V8 handy.

About the Author

Todd Strasser has written many award-winning novels for young and teenage readers. Among his best-known books are *Help! I'm Trapped in Obedience School* and *Help! I'm Trapped in Santa's Body*. His most recent books for Scholastic are *Help! I'm Trapped in My Lunch Lady's Body* and *Help! I'm Trapped in a Professional Wrestler's Body*.

The movie *Next to You*, starring Melissa Joan Hart, was based on the novel *How I Created My Perfect Prom Date*.

Todd speaks frequently at schools about the craft of writing and conducts writing workshops for young people. He and his family live outside New York City with their yellow Labrador retriever, Mac.

You can find out more about Todd and his books at http://www.toddstrasser.com